MAKAN

By Evan Couchot

NOVELS:

Makan

Adverse Events (coming 2026)

NOVELLAS:

Insatiable

MAKAN

Evan Couchot

Makan

Published by Crypsis Press LLC

Stoneham, Massachusetts

www.crypsispress.com

Cover Design by Justin Couchot

First Edition: February 2026

ISBN: 978-1-971827-03-2 (paperback)

ISBN: 978-1-971827-02-5 (ebook)

Library of Congress Control Number: 2026902498

MAKAN

1

"Marc," First Minister Aran Shen said as he walked in through the Garden's double doors with a somber expression. He was a little taller than Marc, in a modern, charcoal-colored suit. His face was aged and his hair was icy silver. "There's been another one." Marc Morrison looked up from his notes to meet his gaze with confusion.

"A fourth?" Marc asked. First Minister Shen nodded gravely. "Where did he die, Aran?"

"She," he corrected, "died in the Elombe Station. Collapsed in the middle of a crowd."

"What does Vertellica think?" Marc probed for more information.

"They're looking for answers but haven't drawn any conclusions just yet. They think…" Aran hesitated as his eyes drifted away from Marc.

"They think it's the food?" Marc connected the dots.

"They think it might be." First Minister Shen shifted his weight uncomfortably. "And they want you to look into it." Marc didn't know what to say.

"If you have the time, we can sift through the information in my office," the First Minister filled the silence.

"Just routine maintenance here, nothing my people can't handle without me." Marc walked away from the row of vibrant plants and made his way toward the doors. First Minister Shen strode behind with the air of a politician trying to avoid a tough situation. The two made their way into the Nutricorps lobby. The young, dark-haired receptionist sat in the center of the room at a desk adorning the company logo.

"Ashley, I'm stepping out for the day. Let me know if Greg comes around looking for me."

"Will do, Mr. Morrison," she responded with a smile before looking back at the screen on her desk. Marc and the First Minister proceeded out of the lobby and into the wide atrium of Government Center. The long, wide hall with an abundance of large doors housed the offices for most of the local businesses. It was lined by slick metal walls. The ceiling was what always kept Marc's attention. Since moving here, he couldn't help but look up. It was entirely glass, revealing all the stars in the expanse above. The sun was down, yet the hall was completely lit by the lights in the walls.

The two walked silently together while Marc remembered his first view of this planet. He thought back to the long flight from Earth, just him and a few other passengers. All of which were natives of the Makan Colony that worked for Vertellica. The month-long journey was not made available to anyone outside their organization. Except for Marc.

The curved windows of the aircraft had adjusted their light filters, allowing for clear sights of the new world. The landscape held little color. There was no green. There was no blue. What shade variations existed were all different browns and tans. Mountain ranges spiked out of the ground contrasting the widespread vein-like canyons. Flat expanses of desert took what area was left. It was reminiscent of the traveling he did in his younger days, getting passed by people left and right while climbing the jutting canyon rocks back home. Marc pushed the memories out of his head.

First Minister Shen boarded a car on the magnet rail as Marc followed. The car was a slim, elongated capsule, with two rows of seats facing each other. Once they were settled, it smoothly accelerated towards Elombe Station. After their arrival, they switched tracks to proceed to the residential zone.

Soon they arrived at First Minister Shen's residence and waited for the dull buzzing sound that indicated that the door was unlocked. The two exited the magnet car as the door slid open. They entered the entry room for the First Minister's residence. It was a large room with a crystal chandelier lighting the beet red walls. There was a waterfall flowing down one wall and into a black rock well. Marc recognized the smell of the air, somehow a little crisper than his own apartment. It was a beautiful place, fitting for the political head of the colony.

"Anything to drink?" First Minister Shen asked Marc as he approached a shelf with several amber bottles and glasses.

"No, thank you," came Marc's response. He proceeded to the office in the next room. A familiar setting that he had sat in many times over the past year, getting to know the colony and its inner workings through First Minister Shen's eyes. He helped Marc to adjust after his arrival and the two became good friends.

The First Minister filed into the room after Marc, holding a glass of dark brown liquid. Ice crystals coated the glass except where his fingers moved. The two stood over a squared desk, looking at the digital display of information. Marc swiped through the data.

"She was only 84," he commented as he continued through the late woman's biographical information.

"Yes," came the First Minister's reply. "It was definitely an early death." He took a sip from his glass as he read over Marc's shoulder. His fingers moved around the screen as he brought up more and more data.

"She had an annual checkup with her physician just a few days ago. They recorded her nutrient levels from a blood sample. I'm not a physician, but there don't seem to be any kind of vitamin or mineral imbalances." Marc looked over at First Minister Shen. "Vertellica thinks it's the food source?"

"I'm afraid so, Marc," the First Minister answered. "But that could just be the Head of Vertellica stirring up trouble like he does sometimes. Just give it some thought over the next day or so. Hopefully we can gather more information by then." He sat in a cloth padded chair next to the desk.

Marc gave up his search and took a seat across from First Minister Shen. He sat in silence as he analyzed the situation. The First Minister took another drink and waited for Marc to gather his thoughts. The only sound was the dull humming of the desk screen as it continued to display information.

"I just don't understand why this keeps happening, Aran," Marc finally said. "That's what, four deaths since I got here a year ago? No known cause, all fairly early compared to the average life expectancy."

"Five if you count your reason for coming in the first place," First Minister Shen added. Marc nodded. "We desperately needed a new agritechnologist after the death of our last one."

"Five," Marc said quietly to himself, letting himself remember the unfortunate situation that brought him to his current position at Nutricorps. Death in old age was expected. Everyone knew that despite having genetic disease predispositions removed, the body still breaks down after a certain point, though much later than in past generations. "I don't get it."

"Remember, Marc," First Minister Shen began to reassure him. "The Makan Colony is the first and only one of its kind. Designed as a hub from which we can explore greater distances into space in the hopes of finding habitable planets. We're coming up on our 6-score anniversary soon. We're still in our infancy. Everyone that lives here now was born here." He took a final sip to empty his glass, which was now dripping with condensation. "Aside from you, of course." He corrected himself as he tipped his drink towards Marc.

"I know," Marc let some of his worry drift away with the First Minister's finished sentence. "I just keep trying to figure out the difference between Earth and here. And why in such a small population there have been so many unexplained deaths. Everything leads me back to one thing."

"Yes, the oxygen level here is lower than on Earth." First Minister Shen knew where Marc's thoughts were going. He had expressed similar concerns related to plant growth in the Garden a few times.

"You still don't think it could be related?" Marc asked.

"If it was, don't you think we would have many more incidents just like the one today?"

"Maybe," Marc paused. "It's hard to tell."

"People have been living here for years without problems up until more recently. The people here are adapted to this lifestyle because they've lived it their entire lives." The First Minister continued. "Do you remember why we have lower oxygen levels in the first place?"

"Because when they built everything here underground, they were worried that the oxygen supplies would be prone to combustion if they came into contact with the planet's atmosphere." Marc grew up learning about the development of the Makan Colony. He had never imagined that one day he would be there.

"Yes, so the brilliant minds at Vertellica," First Minister Shen added with a sarcastic tone. "Decided that dropping the oxygen percentage from 21 percent like on Earth, down to 19 percent would be much safer and require smaller storage systems. They did many studies and determined that adapting people to the lower level during their journey here was safe."

"Yeah, well you know how their readings really were." Marc prodded the First Minister with a smirk.

"Yes, I know," First Minister Shen continued. "They had faulty atmosphere readings that meant combustion wasn't actually a reasonable risk to mitigate. But people had already been living here for over a decade when they figured out their mistake. At that point it would've been more dangerous to raise the oxygen levels rather than keep them the same." He shook his head. Vertellica was initially a pharmaceutical company that was very good at advancing healthcare, but slower to produce results in other sectors. It was one of the largest corporations in history and funded the development for the Makan Colony.

"They do make their mistakes now and then," Marc added, both of their moods lightened thinking about Vertellica's blunders.

"Though it must've been a difficult task, correctly characterizing every single detail of a planet that's in a different solar system." First Minister Shen always played the politician, trying to credit everyone and be liked by all. But he added a wink at the end reminding Marc how he really felt. Marc had heard him talk about the stubbornness and non-cooperation of Vertellica many times.

"You know," Marc began to change the subject. "There's actually a plant that was discovered within the last few decades called *Rafflesia*—"

"—*aerobia*." First Minister Shen finished his sentence.

"Have I mentioned this before?" Marc asked as he cocked his head.

"Your favorite rare plant? One that was discovered in the most secluded microenvironment on Earth? That sprouts yellow and purple star-shaped flowers when grown in an abundance of oxygen?" First Minister Shen asked rhetorically. "No, I don't think you've mentioned it."

The two men laughed together.

"You know what I'm saying," Marc said, still smiling. "Small oxygen differences have negative effects on one living thing, so I'm always going to be hesitant to admit that it doesn't have at least some small impact on human health."

"I understand what you mean, Marc, but I assure you, in this case Vertellica didn't make a mistake." The First Minister seemed confident.

Marc nodded, still unconvinced.

"Well, it's getting late," Marc said as he stood. "I should get going."

"Maybe a drink next time then?" First Minister Shen arose after Marc.

"Yes, definitely. Assuming our meeting is under better circumstances."

"I hope so," the First Minister responded. "Hopefully soon you'll be caught up with the mess that was left behind for you at Nutricorps." The colony was without an experienced agritechnologist for a few months before Marc's arrival, so he had to reestablish the sustainability of the Garden. A process that Marc had found daunting and, at times, overwhelming.

"Almost there," Marc said. "Pretty soon the Garden will practically take care of itself." He smiled at the thought.

"Then maybe you'll finally be able to spend some time in the recreation center and decompress. I'm sure your first time there should be fun." First Minister Shen walked him out and toward the magnet rail.

"I've been there a couple times," Marc said defensively.

"Have you?" The First Minister displayed playful skepticism.

"But it would be nice to actually know what drinks to order and maybe figure out how Hexball works," Marc admitted with a shrug.

The First Minister chuckled as he opened the entrance to the magnet car. His mind wandered thinking about Hexball, the sport that was born in the Makan Colony.

"You bring up oxygen levels as the major difference between Earth and here. But that's not the only one. What about gravity?" First Minister Shen asked.

"I thought about that initially, this planet being so much smaller than Earth and all. I even talked to a few other agritechs before I came." Marc began to explain. "The gravity here is only 8 percent less than on Earth so it doesn't really affect nutrient carrying in plants. It actually may make it easier because osmosis often has to fight gravity. I never really understood how such a small planet can have similar gravity to Earth." Marc thought to himself.

"I understand. I thought it could be worth thinking about but I guess you beat me to it."

"Thank you for your hospitality, as always, Aran," Marc said as he began to enter the car.

"You're always welcome," the First Minister responded. "Oh and Marc, the answer to your question is the density."

Marc nodded as he proceeded into the car and waved his goodbye as the door sealed shut behind him.

Marc got off the magnet rail and noticed it was darker in this zone than at First Minister Shen's residence. He glanced at the lights where the wall met the ceiling and observed a more orangish hue than before. They followed their typical light patterns to simulate normal Earth daylight schedules. The colony was, after all, entirely underground. The days and nights on the surface were longer than those back on Earth.

Marc approached his apartment door. There was no handle, no lock, and no key necessary. He thought back to the first time he used it. His receptionist, Ashley, had picked him up in Elombe Station to show him to his apartment after he arrived. She gave a brief tour filled with excited yet nervous rambling.

He remembered reluctantly asking her for help opening the door after she had already turned away to leave. And of course he could still picture her giggling as she explained something that was so ingrained into her daily life. It didn't help the anxious feelings he already had for his first few moments on the new planet.

Marc placed his right palm on the door and it slid to the side quickly. The lights in the apartment flicked on when he walked in. He entered with the kitchen to the left and a closet to the right. The kitchen was relatively small with dark metal cabinets and some kind of a lightly speckled, orange rock countertop.

There was a collection of small plants lining the back edge of the counter. Marc examined each one as he walked past. He saw blooming chrysanthemums, healthy snake plants and ivies, as well as a simple ferocactus. At the end of the row was an empty pot of soil. *Rafflesia aerobia,* Marc noted while fingering the loose dirt. *I never could get you to grow in this air.* He brushed off his hand with a twinge of disappointment.

Marc continued walking in and found himself in the living room, furnished with a wall screen, a gray couch, and circular end tables with orange tinted glass tops on either side. There was a small metal coffee table in front of the couch that seemed too low to be functional. When he got close enough, the wall screen turned on to reveal looping videos of rolling green hills. *Not something I'll see here,* Marc thought.

He then walked left from the living room and down a short hallway with a door on both sides and a picture frame showing two beautiful children he didn't know. He hadn't yet taken the time to replace the stock photos. On his left was the washroom and on his right was his bedroom.

It was a simple bedroom. Not tiny but far from big. Marc was always relieved by the carpet after his long days on his feet at Nutricorps. He crawled into his bed, exhaling deeply as he got comfortable. The lights faded away as he fell asleep.

2

Marc woke to sunlight shining on his face. Standard timing meant that it was six. Time to get up. He got out of bed, still dressed from the day before and headed into the washroom. After cleaning himself up, he dressed in his Nutricorps uniform.

Marc foraged around the kitchen, finding some breakfast. He sat down to eat when the counter lit up to reveal a screen.

"...First Minister Aran Shen stated this morning that the rumors surrounding the changes to gene editing procedures in the colony were false." A reporter was looking at him through the counter. "He said, 'The idea to remove restrictions on genetic enhancements in the Makan Colony is ridiculous. Every day I fight for our rights to remain natural, just as I believe Elombe and our citizens would want.'" The reporter looked up from her notebook. "You heard it here first."

Marc thought about why he was sitting in this kitchen, millions of miles away from the planet on which he had grown up. He had lived here for about a year, but sometimes it still felt as if he had just arrived. He felt optimistic about the change while reflecting on his previous life. Marc was born a product of IVF, just like everyone had been for decades. Screening and removal of disease predispositions were of course performed but he wasn't fortunate enough to get any enhancements. His parents couldn't afford it.

Genetic editing, outside of disease prevention, was illegal in the Makan Colony. The government wanted natural gene lines present as humans continue to branch out across the universe.

Marc was about halfway through his bowl of cereal. It tasted similar to the stuff he grew up eating as a child. The major difference was the taste of plant-based milk. There were no livestock in the colony, after all.

He finished his meal and stood up from the counter. The screen in the countertop shut off and the lights followed as

Marc walked out the door on his way to work. This time it slid open without trouble.

He made his way back to Elombe Station. He wanted to walk around the place and see if there was anything unusual about the woman's death the previous day. The place opened into a large concourse with a few magnet rails on the back wall. He glided down the moving stairs and landed in the middle of the room.

Glancing around and watching the crowd hustle and bustle he felt extraordinarily average. He wasn't short. He wasn't overweight. He was surrounded by all shapes and sizes, all shades and proportions. Even after all his time here it still felt unfamiliar to him after growing up around the seemingly perfect crowds of beautiful Earth natives.

In the center of the space stood a massive golden statue of a man. The man held two books against his chest and was looking upward at an angle while sporting a subtle smile. Marc walked up to it and examined the name plate that rested below the statue's feet. *Elombe Nkulu - Conceptor of the Makan Colony.* He recognized the man from the stories about the colony's creation. He was originally a philosopher obsessed with religion and human development. He was the one who convinced Vertellica, along with some of the other major corporations on Earth, to expand our reach deep into space. Together they created the World Organization for Space Exploration, or WOSE. Their goal was, as Elombe phrased it, the best hope to avoid the inevitabilities of global destruction and human extinction. WOSE also was tasked with establishing and maintaining the political system of the Makan Colony.

Marc passed by a small group of people, all dressed in green uniforms with innumerable pockets. Stunners sat on their hips. Marc recognized them as WOSE security. They stood around a small roped-off area, inside of which there were a few orange-clad Vertellica scientists investigating the scene. They had already removed the body.

Marc looked around the surrounding area for anything unusual. Instead, he found a completely normal section of Elombe Station. Whatever happened, it wasn't caused by the location. *Maybe she had an undiagnosed underlying condition?* Marc pondered. He decided to end his investigation and rely on the notes he would later receive from Vertellica.

Marc followed his footsteps back to the magnet rails and headed to Nutricorps.

While walking down the deceptively long hall of Government Center, Marc passed the usual doors. Each one with an illuminated plate with the corporation or department name. He passed the doors for Leto's Best, the company in charge of maintaining the colony's water supply. They also made a variety of soft and hard drinks. Next, he passed the Waste Management Department. Their work wasn't glamorous, but it was important nonetheless. Finally he came to the door for Nutricorps. Unsurprisingly, there was a succulent suspended in a pot above the door.

As Marc walked up to the door it slid open to reveal a waiting room with Ashley sitting at her chest-height desk. The Nutricorps logo was backlit and glowing on the front of the desk. Two bonsai trees, immaculately maintained, sat on each side of the desk.

"Hi Ashley." Her head was down but lifted quickly when she heard her name.

"Good morning, Mr. Morrison!" She seemed surprised to see Marc. "I'll message Mr. Andino to tell him you're here. I think he wanted to speak to you."

"Sounds good, thanks." Marc proceeded through the door to Ashley's right and sat down at his desk. Beyond his desk, the scent of plants and the humidity from the Garden filled the air.

There was a sudden tapping on Marc's metallic name plate on the wall across from his desk.

"Marc! How are you today?" Greg Andino came into his office smiling. He was a cheery, bespectacled man who was more than slightly overweight for his height. He worked for Nutricorps on the operations side, while Marc handled everything from the scientific perspective. Greg was the head of all of Nutricorps, therefore making him Marc's boss.

"I'm doing alright, all things considered," Marc answered.

"C'mon, let's walk and talk." He turned and nodded his head in the direction of the Garden. Marc followed.

After passing through the other office spaces, the building opened up into what looked like a warehouse. It was open, yet there were green, translucent hallways scattered everywhere. It was the greatest engineering feat within the colony. Acres and acres of space with vertical growth systems to maximize the utility of every centimeter.

"I heard that First Minister Shen approached you about the woman that died in Elombe Station yesterday."

"Yes, he did," Marc responded. "He had me look over some of the woman's information to see if I could find anything unusual. I guess Vertellica is suspicious that it has something to do with the food we're growing."

"I spoke to a few of the investigators with WOSE and Vertellica about it," Greg added. "Like you mentioned, they don't really know the cause of death. I'm sure First Minister Shen gave you the similar talk saying 'we don't think it's the food but we want to consider every option.'" Greg rolled his eyes.

"I got the more direct version but more or less the same contents," Marc commented. "I'll look through everything today and see if I find anything unusual."

"Don't be surprised if you don't find anything, Marc," Greg said. "These Vertellica guys, they tend to always look outward rather than inward when there's a problem." He finished his explanation as he altered course to head back to Marc's office.

"It was the same back on Earth," Marc said. "But they had less control of everything back there."

"They're good people, though. Hell, I grew up with most of them. They just see things through orange-tinted lenses, rather than from the general human perspective."

"Everyone has different colored lenses, Greg. The trick is to know which color goes with which people." Marc grew up skeptical. Much of his childhood was spent around genetically enhanced people that looked down on him. But he knew they all looked from different angles.

"First Minister Shen said you were the best of the best when you were brought here. Our last agritechnologist wasn't that bright. He thought squash were vegetables and carrots were fruit." Greg smiled and winked at Marc. Then he paused uncomfortably. "I don't mean to talk bad about the dead but you know what I mean."

"I know what you mean," Marc reassured him with a laugh. "I was grateful for the opportunity to come here, but it could've been under better circumstances."

Greg nodded. The two had arrived back at Marc's office. Greg's eyes wandered around it as Marc took a seat at his desk.

"Hundreds of lives depend on your ability to grow fruit. Did you ever think that would be the case? I sure as hell wouldn't want to be in that position." He looked at Marc laughing again.

"So you've mentioned," Marc responded, laughing along with discomfort.

"You know, you have a lot of room here, Marc. You ought to decorate and make it more homey."

"I'll get around to it at some point, I'm sure," Marc replied. "You know how busy I've been since I got here."

"I know, I know," He waved his hand dismissively. "Just give it some thought." With that comment, Greg left Marc alone in the office.

Marc went about his work day, checking over the nutrient distribution systems. He found himself wandering through the Garden, speaking with his workers and helping them whenever necessary.

After a while, Marc wandered around lost in thought. He had time to appreciate the beauty of the complex system. Almost everything the colony consumes comes from the Garden. All of the plants here are essential to life. Triticum, vulgare, legumes of all sorts, tons of fruits and vegetables.

He walked through the rows and rows of various plants towards the back side of the warehouse. The changing smells and humidity while walking through each row was complex and shifting. Pipes that supplied nutrient-spiked water to the plants were hidden under the floor panels, moving around like neurons in the brain. Each sending very specific contents to specialized sections of vegetation.

The area was so large that the walls of the room looked to be miles away through the misty air. Passing through row after row, examining plant after plant. He felt a temperature gradient changing as he progressed through the Garden. Grains, vegetables, fruits, roots, tubers, more grains, legumes. Most strains engineered. Few strains that were truly natural. He walked by row after row of intragenus grafts. Plants used to maintain multiple varieties of produce yet only on one plant. It was the most advanced agritech facility Marc had ever worked in.

He touched healthy leaves and fruit as he moved towards the Garden's lab. It was along one wall of the massive space. There were pH meters, a spectrophotometer, a gas chromatograph, hydrometers, dispersion analyzers, scales, and anything else Marc could ever need. When he arrived here for the first time, he made special equipment requests which Vertellica had handled efficiently.

Greg was fantastic at working with the other corporations to achieve common goals. He guaranteed Marc that he could get him any piece of equipment he wanted. Of course, when equipment appeared, some of the higher quality produce coincidentally disappeared.

Seeing the lab gave Marc an idea. He circled the forests around him until he returned back to his office space. Sitting back down, he dove into the suite of applications on his desk display.

He tapped around on the screen until he found what he was looking for. An application with an emblem of three arrows which swirled parallel to each other. Looking through the program, he found the readings for the current air composition in the Garden.

Marc took more notes:

```
Nitrogen 79.22%, Oxygen 17.40%, Ar-
gon  0.97%,  Carbon  Dioxide  0.42%,
Trace Elements 0.99%.
```

Marc read back through the notes. *I must've made a mistake,* he thought. *Oxygen at 17.40 percent?* He checked again. Sure enough, that's what the reading was.

Standing up from his desk and leaving the office space, Marc made his way through the Garden and back to the lab. He grabbed a few test tubes and found iron shreddings in a drawer under the lab bench. He filled up the test tubes with water, and added the shreddings to half of the tubes to run an iron oxidation test. It was a simple chemistry experiment he had learned as a child. Marc inverted the tubes while sealed and went back to his desk.

Surely, the desk application was wrong, he thought. On Earth, oxygen makes up 21 percent of the air in the atmosphere. The Makan Colony has operated at 19 percent for over 100 years, but this was even lower than that. He had calculated new nutrient balances based on the expected 19 percent. Marc knew that for plants, a slightly lower amount wouldn't be detrimental. After all, they undergo cellular respiration at much lower levels than animals and take in most of their oxygen in the form of water. Photosynthesis makes up for the difference. For humans, it's a different story.

The readings have to be wrong.

Marc kept going about his day, checking out other conditions in the Garden. Everything seemed normal, or as normal as a massive agritech system could be. Every half hour he analyzed the water displacement of the iron oxidation tubes until his day was nearing the end.

Marc calculated the air's oxygen saturation based on his experiment and couldn't believe his findings. Oxygen made up 17.40 percent of the air in the Garden.

Briskly walking back to the office spaces, Marc checked for Greg in his office. He wasn't there. He rarely was. His work has him spending time at other facilities more often than at Nutricorps.

Then he looked for Ashley. Walking out into the lobby, Marc discovered that she was still there, using her desk screen.

"Hey Ashley, do you know what the air composition is here?" She looked up from her desk inquisitively and took a moment to process the question.

"I think it's mostly nitrogen and oxygen with a bunch of other elements in smaller amounts." She wasn't wrong, but also didn't seem to know any more of the specifics.

"Yeah, that's pretty much right. Do you know where Greg is?"

"He left early because he has a dinner with Vertellica tonight. If you need him, you can probably call him from your desk. "As always, she was very helpful, but Marc was too focused to acknowledge it verbally.

"Alright," he said as he turned back towards his office.

"Oh and Marc, before Greg left he said he wanted something delivered to you. Do you want me to send it over now?" Ashley asked quickly.

"Sure, Ashley. Thanks," he went back to his desk and found Greg on the audio application. There was a long pause with low humming music.

Finally Greg answered and his face showed on the screen.

"Marc, what can I do for you?" He was clearly walking yet his image was perfectly still.

"Hi Greg, quick question. What's the air composition of the colony?" Marc blurted out the question.

"I'm not sure exactly, but I know it's roughly 78 percent nitrogen, 19 percent, oxygen, one percent..."

"Has it always ever been lower than 19 percent oxygen?" Marc had to interrupt.

"I'm sure there are fluctuations here and there," Greg gave a slight laugh, muffled with confusion. Marc didn't say anything. He didn't know what to say.

"Is everything alright?" Greg asked.

"I'm not sure. I was just checking the air composition in the Garden and it showed lower levels." Marc was still confused.

"How low are you talking here, Marc?" His eyebrows narrowed as he looked at Marc through the screen.

"About one point six percent."

"One point six percent! Jeez Marc! That's peanuts. There's barely a difference and you made it seem like life as you know it was changed." He bellowed with heavy laughter. "Alright then. Need anything else while you have me? It's probably about quitting time for the day isn't it?"

"That's all I wanted to check on," Marc said, a little calmer now because of Greg's reaction. "We can talk more about it when you're back. Take care."

"Sounds great, gotta get home to the wife and kids before I leave again for dinner. See you in the Garden," Greg ended the conversation.

Marc checked the time on his desk screen. He was right. It was 15 minutes past the end of Marc's work day. He wrote one final note on his desk screen and circled it before getting up to leave: *Low oxygen??*

"Mr. Morrison, there's a delivery for you. Sending her back now," Ashley's voice came through the speaker on Marc's desk.

"Thanks, Ashley," Marc responded, pressing the button on his desk to allow his voice to go through.

The door near his office space opened up revealing a face Marc recognized but didn't yet know personally. It was a pleasant one. A woman in a gray shirt and pants strutted in carrying a dark metal pot. She smiled and her maple hair bounced while approaching Marc. A golden name tag was displayed on the left side of her chest. *Lian*. First Minister Shen's daughter. She handled most of the deliveries throughout the Makan Colony.

"Hi, delivery for Marc?" her voice was soothing. Marc stood up to take the pot and looked up to meet her hazel eyes.

"That was quick." He commented. "Thank you."

"It's a small colony," she responded pleasantly. "I'm Lian by the way, we haven't officially met."

"It's nice to meet you, Lian." Marc smiled as they shook hands.

"You too, Marc."

"What is this?" He inspected the tiny stem within the pot.

"I think Greg said it was a rainbow sequoia." She responded, smiling.

"Interesting. I've never grown one of these before. Thanks!" Marc looked up from the plant and smiled back at Lian. It was a unique gift to say the least. Marc had never even seen one in person. Not until now. It was almost enough to distract him from his oxygen confusion.

"Any time. See you around." Then she turned and walked back out the door, continuing with her deliveries. She had no scars, no birthmarks, no abnormalities of any kind, yet she still seemed unique. Marc was lost in her beauty. And he noted that she was surprisingly tall.

"Bye," Marc said.

He noticed a small note in the pot next to the stem.

```
Marc, I got this rainbow sequoia from
the guys at Vertellica. Thought it
might take your mind off the events
yesterday.
```

Marc smiled as he carried the plant away from his office. He waved goodbye to Ashley as he walked out of the Nutricorps front doors.

On his way home, Marc walked by some of the other industries in this wing of the colony. He passed by ProFusion, the company that maintains the colony power systems. Then the Fabrication Corporation. They can turn anything into something useful. The last notable facility Marc passed by was the orange entrance for Vertellica. Anywhere that needs medicine has a Vertellica facility. The next door he passed was also labeled for Vertellica. They funded most of the colony, so it made sense that they worked out a deal to get every facility they wanted.

He made the short trek back to his apartment for the night with his new roommate. Once Marc was back, he set the small plant on the counter in line with his other plants. He crept over and plopped down on the couch. The wall screen flashed on. It was more news about the government in the colony. Politics was never anything Marc found particularly interesting. He grabbed the remote touchpad to change channels.

Flipping through the guide revealed a channel called E.H. He switched to it to see what it was all about. The screen began to display animals and plants from Earth. *I bet they have 21 percent oxygen*. Marc shook his head. After watching for a short amount of time, the unabbreviated title was revealed in the bottom corner of the screen. It read *Evolutionary Home.*

Marc laid back and continued to watch until his eyelids eventually slid shut, and he fell asleep.

3

The following day Marc went about his usual work until lunch. When it came time, he returned to First Minister Shen's residence for their weekly meal. There was a dull buzzing sound and the door slid open.

Marc got out of the car and walked through the door into a familiar setting with a crystal chandelier. Footsteps echoed through the vast room.

"Marc! Welcome!" he said while approaching. He grinned cheek to cheek and his perfect teeth sparkled in the light of the chandelier.

He reminded Marc of all the classically handsome men he grew up around. The ones that got all the girls and were always successful in everything they did. *At least the First Minister was from the colony so it's natural and not paid for,* Marc thought.

"How are you, Aran?" Marc asked.

"I'm famished. Been looking forward to this meal all morning."

"You and me both."

The two passed through a nearby door and into the dining room. The furniture was beautiful stone, with elegant glass plates, cups, and eating utensils set for two.

"When you get to my age, good meals make all the difference in a great day," First Minister Shen said.

Marc smiled in acknowledgment. From afar it was difficult to tell how old the First Minister was, but when Marc was close he could see the well-hidden lines on his face. Even through his handsomeness, it was evident in the way he moved and stared at Marc's mouth when listening.

They were standing on opposite sides of the dining table. First Minister Shen pulled out his chair and took a seat. Marc followed suit at a wave of his host's arm.

"So, Aran," Marc began. "Has Vertellica figured out any new information about the woman's death?"

"I wish I had more news, Marc. But unfortunately, they haven't come up with anything yet. They still seem to think there's a chance that it's related to the Garden. If you ask me, I think she was just old."

"That's too bad," Marc said. He was unsure of when to bring up the low oxygen levels.

A man came bustling into the room carrying a clear tray. He dropped off a basket of various rolls and a tray of plant butter before vanishing again.

"Help yourself," First Minister Shen smiled as he grabbed a roll and used a small knife to spread the plant-based butter.

Marc grabbed a molasses roll and First Minister Shen passed the butter his way. Marc spread the butter and took a bite of the doughy mass.

"I saw a story about you today," Marc said between bites. "Something about allowing genetic enhancements in the colony."

"Oh that," he responded with a sigh of concealed annoyance. "That's nothing. It was all just a rumor someone started. There are no genetic enhancements here, Marc. And as long as I'm First Minister, there never will be. I like our people to be adaptable." He winked at Marc.

"I'm glad to hear it. Any idea who started the rumor?"

"Yes, unfortunately I know exactly who started it. It was Lian." The First Minister looked at Marc and shook his head in disapproval.

"Why would she do that?" Marc asked.

"Who knows. She has a habit of starting rumors about me that make people uncomfortable. I always end up doing damage control and eliminating people's worries but it's extra work I wish I didn't have to do."

"Is there a reason behind it, if you don't mind me asking?" Marc wondered.

"She's just stubborn sometimes, and often acts without thinking," First Minister Shen explained. "I know she doesn't actually mean any harm to me. She has an interesting take on jokes."

"I see," Marc responded, unsure of what to say.

"So how is everything going at Nutricorps?" First Minister Shen asked as Marc took a bite.

Marc tried to speed up his chewing, so as not to be rude and talk with his mouth full. Somehow he felt like that made him chew even slower. He finally swallowed the bread.

"Everything is going well. I've caught up to speed and the Garden is more efficient than I've ever seen it."

"Great! It sounds like you're going to deliver on the high expectations that got you here." He paused to take a small bite, swallowed, and continued speaking. "I've never really asked, but is there anything different about the setup here compared to the ones you worked with on Earth?"

"It's pretty similar, but slightly more automated than what I'm used to," Marc looked up from his roll to make the eye contact he had previously broken. "The plants are all the same as on Earth, and they share similar growth patterns. Even after I had to adjust for the lower oxygen level."

"Oh yes, I'm sure that finding out our air contains less oxygen than you're used to must've been somewhat shocking," First Minister Shen said. "Has there been a significant effect on the plants?"

"I haven't seen any major negative effects since the plants get the oxygen needed for respiration from their water, but time will tell how it affects their cellular homeostasis. I had to adjust the nutrient and water supplies for each individual species, but not by a lot," Marc admitted.

"That's good to hear. The effect of lower oxygen levels on humans was obviously very well studied before the colony decided on an appropriate percentage. 19 percent. That was the final determination. Of course, that was well before I was making the decisions." He concluded as the waiter came back through the door to pick up the empty breadbasket and the butter.

"Yes, well you're not quite 120 years old. But slowly getting there." Marc joked.

"Yes, yes. Laugh at the old man," the First Minister smiled. "I've always lived a more active life than others my age."

"I can attest to that. You're all over this colony," Marc added.

"Age won't slow me down; I won't let it. Though I have started to take more and more meetings here, as opposed to the WOSE office."

"You weren't young when you had Lian, either."

"You've got that right. Nowadays…"

"You mean back in the day," Marc chided. The First Minister rolled his eyes.

"As I was saying, for the last century people haven't needed to have kids at the biologically optimal age. As the general cost of living continued to rise, it was harder and harder. The universality of IVF made it less of an issue. I could have a child in my 60's and scientists could remove any damaged or mutated DNA and replace it with normal versions. Even better than normal."

"I know what you mean," Marc commented. "In your 60's? So that makes Lian…"

"About your age," First Minister Shen finished his sentence. "She told me that you two met today."

"Yes, I'm shocked it took until yesterday to meet her."

"You don't get deliveries to Nutricorps often?" The First Minister probed.

"We do but Ashley or Greg usually take care of them," Marc answered.

"I see. She's a spitting image of her mother, you know." The man looked to the side thoughtfully.

"Is she?"

"Absolutely," First Minister Shen said. "The only problem she has is that she's grown up with too much attention."

"I can understand why," Marc grabbed at his water glass to take a drink.

"Excuse me?" The First Minister's expression changed. Marc almost choked on his water.

"Well, she makes deliveries all over the colony," Marc said defensively. "I'm sure she talks to a lot of people."

The First Minister looked at him suspiciously but moved on.

They paused their conversation while the server came in and dropped off plates of food in front of each of them. It was a green salad, with various beans and rice mixed in.

"Recognize any of these plants?" First Minister Shen joked as he picked up the dressing decanter to smother his salad.

"There is something I wanted to talk to you about," Marc began. "I took some readings in the Garden yesterday."

"And?" He passed Marc the dressing.

"Well, the oxygen level is lower than expected."

"Yes, we've talked about it being at 19 percent rather than the 21 percent of Earth," The First Minister responded calmly as he ate his salad.

"It's lower than that," Marc said in a serious tone. First Minister Shen set down his fork.

"How low is it?" First Minister Shen's face showed concern as his brows furrowed.

"17.4 percent. 1.6 percent lower than expected."

"17.4 percent," the First Minister hesitated. "Did you tell anyone else about this?"

"I told Greg about it but he didn't seem to think it was a big deal."

"That's good," First Minister Shen said quietly. He seemed deep in thought.

"Good?" Marc asked.

"Well, we don't want to induce panic, especially in the non-scientist population."

"Do you think this is a panic worthy situation?" Marc examined the calm face across from him but could tell there was a lot going on in his head.

"It's hard to say, but for now let's keep this between us. I'll speak to the folks over at Vertellica later today and see what's going on." He called over the man that was serving their food and told him to set up a meeting. The man nodded and quickly walked away.

"Let me know what you find out," Marc said. "If it's something I need to adjust for in the Garden then I'd like that information sooner than later. Not to mention if it has the potential to negatively affect people."

"Yes, of course. I'll keep you updated." The First Minister continued to eat. "Hopefully everything works out for the best."

"Did you read the studies about the impact of lower oxygen levels on humans?" Marc was curious about the potential negative effects. He assumed there must be some.

"I read them a long time ago. I'd let you borrow them if I had them, but Vertellica keeps a tight lock on all of their data. Not sure why, they seem to think that someone could steal their business here in the colony," First Minister Shen said. "That's not going to happen."

"Do you remember what you read?" Marc wanted to stay on track. It didn't surprise him that Vertellica had the information. They were a scientific powerhouse for over two centuries back on Earth.

"I remember very vaguely, but it has been a long time," the First Minister admitted.

"And what do you remember?" Marc prodded.

"Decreased oxygen levels in the brain tend to limit function, especially during development. The effect has less impact after the brain is fully developed in adulthood." He said this in a tone that Marc found alarmingly casual.

"What?!" Marc exclaimed.

"That wasn't every case though, Marc," First Minister Shen explained. "If I remember right, that was the effect of drastically lowering the oxygen levels in a short time period. Something like instantly dropping people into 15 percent oxygen and seeing what happened."

"They did these experiments on people?"

"No, no. I misspoke. They used model organisms. Mice and rats. I think some non-human primates too. I know that the 19 percent oxygen was decided on because it was completely safe according to their experiments. I think it even gave a small buffer percentage. We're probably still in that acceptable range. And people do adapt, of course."

Marc gave a sigh of relief. The First Minister could tell that he was still skeptical.

"Think about it, Marc. If people on the Makan Colony had less oxygen their entire lives, and doing so would affect their brain development, don't you think you would've noticed?" he posed an important question.

"I suppose there would probably be some level of intellectual impairment," Marc concluded. "But everyone seems normal."

"Exactly, if that were true, you would walk around here like a God. Even if there was a slight risk of any kind of harm to humans, that was over 100 years ago. People surely would have adapted over time."

First Minister Shen saw Marc running thoughts through his mind as he took slow bites of the meal. Aran was nearly finished eating. Marc looked down at his own plate. There was barely a dent.

"I suppose so, though evolution is a long process," Marc said.

"That it is, Marc. If only science could crack that one." First Minister Shen smiled at the thought. Then he knocked on the table and the server hastily walked in, grabbed their empty plates, and hurried back out the door.

"That'll be some day," Marc agreed.

Their server came back in and whispered into the First Minister's ear and walked away. He stood up from his seat.

"It looks like Vertellica is fitting me in right away."

Marc stood up from his seat as the First Minister motioned his arm towards the door. Dinner was coming to an end. It wasn't Marc's favorite meal, there was no real protein besides the beans. That was something he knowingly accepted when coming to the colony.

Marc walked half a step back, on the right side of the First Minister as he led back out of his dining room and towards the magnet car.

During the walk Marc noticed an opening to a darker room with orange lighting that seemed to be lined with bookshelves. *How could he get so many books here?* Marc asked himself. By now he had come to the realization that almost everything in the colony was digital, so this was even more shocking.

"Thank you for lunch," Marc said, looking back at the First Minister as he climbed into the car.

"I was happy for the company and the conversation, though hopefully our next one is about much more positive topics."

"Agreed," Marc responded.

"Oh Marc, everything going on lately seems like a lot. Maybe since you're caught up in the Garden you should take up a hobby to take your mind off things. Maybe get a Blockade board," First Minister Shen spoke his final words as the doors sealed shut in the middle.

The car stalled on the track, and after waiting a minute or two, it finally began to move towards his residential zone. The car moved with such force that Marc coughed from the pressure.

Marc traveled back to his quiet apartment, all the while contemplating his previous discussion. When walking in, he saw his rainbow sequoia on the kitchen counter. It had grown a tiny amount, with no visible flowering yet. Marc picked it up and held it under the sink to give it a drink.

After watering his little growing tree, he sat down at the counter to think. His eyes moved towards his bowl of germinating seeds. *Still nothing from my Rafflesia aerobia seeds.* He rested his elbows on the counter and held his head up in his hands.

Marc's mind continued to race thinking about what First Minister Aran had said. Could the lower oxygen level be impacting people's development? He wondered. Could it be related to the woman's death, or even the previous ones?

These thoughts rolled around in Marc's head until his cerebral exhaustion put him to sleep that night.

4

Marc woke up from a restless night. He tossed and turned, tangling up his seemingly useless blankets. When he arrived at Nutricorps he glanced around his desk looking for the note he left for himself. There was nothing to be found. He rolled his chair back and heard a muffled cracking underneath him. The note had fallen off the desk.

Low oxygen??

Marc moved the note to the top of the desk. It was time for him to do some work, but first he needed something. He left his desk and went through the door into the lobby. Ashley seemed to be distracted by one of the bonsai trees, staring intently at it. She turned towards Marc and blinked rapidly as if waking from a dream.

"Good morning, Mr. Morrison," she said. "How are you?"

"I'm alright, Ashley," he smiled back. "Could you do me a favor?" Her eyebrows rose up slightly.

"Yes, of course!" she responded with a hint of curiosity.

"I know it's not Nutricorps related but is there any way you could get a Blockade board for me?" He thought the First Minister's advice may be good for him.

"Definitely!" she responded.

"Thanks, just drop it off at my desk when you get a chance," Marc headed back towards the Garden as Ashley nodded. *Maybe I'll get to see Lian again when she brings it*, he thought with a smile. Ashley stopped him before he got too far.

"Mr. Morrison?" Marc turned back to face her.

"Yes Ashley?" She looked at him, then the floor. Back at Marc.

"I…" she stuttered. "I don't really have much work."

"Oh, if I see Greg, I'll…" He began to respond.

"Actually, I was wondering if maybe I could help you with some of yours." She interrupted.

Marc paused before responding. He wasn't used to anyone offering to help with agritech. With anything really.

Ashley noticed his hesitation.

"It's fine if you're busy. I just don't get much work up here and I think I might be more helpful if I learn more about the plants." She began to face her desk again.

"Actually, that sounds great." This gave Marc an idea. "I could use your help with some health analyses."

"Yes, anything!" her face lit up. She touched her desk screen rapidly and then stood up. "I just sent a message to Lian so hopefully she'll bring the board by the end of the day."

"Great, thanks." Marc turned and walked through the door back to his desk. Ashley followed closely, carefully stepping in his footprints. "Do you want me to run through the basic systems for the Garden first?"

"That sounds good to me," Ashley responded eagerly.

"Plants have simple needs," Marc began. "Light, which is widely abundant in the Garden in the form of full spectrum bulbs." He pointed above him. The light system provided an almost purple shade to the ceiling throughout Nutricorps.

"The light settings are divided into quadrants based on the light strength and amount of time the different types of plants need for optimum growth." Marc paused to gauge Ashley's understanding.

"Simple enough," Ashley said.

"Next is space. The great thing about the Garden is that there's a lot of space, and the hydroponic systems in place minimize how much space we actually need by resource maximization." Ashley nodded.

"Another key component would be water," Marc continued. "The brilliant minds behind the colony built plenty of plumbing into the Garden so that water could be controlled with ease. One of the last important needs of plants is nutrients. Nutrients come in all forms, especially on a planet with an undeveloped surface and lack of life."

"Other than us," Ashley commented with a smile.

"Good point. Which is why nutrient management is one of the most difficult parts of the job; properly maintaining nutritional balance on this variety of plants is nearly impossible for most people. Nutricorps shares a wall with the Waste Management Department for a reason," Marc explained. "They recycle all of the waste, especially human waste, in order to extract the valuable nutrients to use as fertilizer for the plants. They extract the chemicals that need to be mixed in the right proportions depending on which plants are being worked with."

"Growing food in waste, yum," Ashley chuckled.

"Luckily we extract the chemicals and leave some stuff behind for other people to deal with," Marc laughed with her before continuing. "Nutrients in the air are also important to plant life. The air contains nitrogen, which is important for nitrogen fixing plants and their mutualists to add back into their environment, as well as oxygen, carbon dioxide, argon, and other less prevalent elements."

"Every day, Waste Management updates what they extract which in turn updates the resources we have available. We usually have an excess because of how efficient the Garden has become."

"That all makes sense to me," Ashley said. "I'm sure I'll learn more about the intricacies as we go."

"You definitely will," Marc responded as he grabbed his digiboard. "The goal today is to go through the Garden and see how healthy the plants are." This was something he did anyway, but he wanted to pay special attention to it today. Marc held out the digiboard for Ashley to see.

"Oh alright," she grabbed the device out of Marc's hand with surprising speed.

"I'm still getting used to the tech here so I tend to go a little slow." Marc rubbed that back of his neck and gave a light chuckle. There was a lot of technology designed specifically for the colony that wasn't in common use back on Earth.

"Wait here, I'll be right back." She disappeared back to her desk.

She came back walk-skipping excitedly. She was carrying her own digiboard.

"This one is synced with my desk, but I can sync it to yours too." She touched around on it and handed it to Marc. "There we go, now it's all set up to sync to both of us."

"Now we're talking about efficiency," Marc said happily as he handed it back.

"Glad I could help!" She was pleased with herself. It was still going to be a lot of work, but now it was much more manageable. "What's next Mr. Morrison?"

"You can call me Marc, Ashley. Mr. Morrison feels too formal."

"Sure thing," she seemed to hesitate. "Marc."

"Are you ready to get started?" Marc asked.

"Yes, of course!" she exclaimed. "I might have to run back to my desk occasionally, but I can definitely help. Can you walk me through a couple rows in the Garden to show me how we check the plants?"

"Definitely. Let's get to it."

They continued to walk down the aisle of legumes, and Ashley carried her digiboard to input the information.

"So you'll notice that every plant is already labeled at the base. It has the type of plant on the top and the species on the bottom of the sign."

Ashley squinted her eyes while bending slightly and then stood up to nod.

"You'll want to compare the color and elasticity of the leaves and stems of each plant to the reference shown on the digiboard." Marc continued as Ashley continued to follow his instructions. "Most of the species within the same type will be given similar nutrient treatments, with some exceptions."

"Do I check the fruit or vegetables themselves too?" Ashley asked. It was a good question.

"Yes, when you get to the fruiting plants, they should have a reference for that on the digiboard page as well. I actually had to learn this stuff without an on-hand reference," Marc said.

"That sounds like a lot of stuff to know without looking at a reference."

"I've been doing this for a long enough time that it helped me a lot to keep it up here," Marc gestured to his head.

They continued down the row.

"So, Ashley," Marc kept the conversation going. "Tell me about yourself." He had been so busy with work over the last year that he hadn't gotten to know her on a personal level.

She paused from her inputting.

"There's not really much to tell," she admitted, thinking she would lose his interest. "I was born and raised here; I went through school with all of the other kids that were my age. After school I worked at the Experience Plaza for a few years. I got bored and then quit to work at the Game Bar. I worked there for a few more years before I realized that I wanted to do something more interesting and complex. I applied for a few of the jobs in Government Center, excluding Vertellica of course, and ended up getting my job here at Nutricorps."

"Why exclude Vertellica?" Marc asked with a smile of confusion. "I'm sure they have tons of different positions."

"It just seems like everyone that works there is the same, you know?" she began. "All just one tiny piece of a bigger whole, none making any of their own decisions."

"I definitely get that, Vertellica controls a lot of things back on Earth. It seems like they have even more power here. What was it like growing up here?"

"It was normal, I guess. I'm not sure what it's like where you're from but here everyone pretty much knows everyone at some level."

"I guess that would be pretty interesting. I grew up in a huge housing complex with thousands of people. I barely knew any of them." Marc paused to think. "I guess comparatively, there are less than two thousand people on this planet and I think there were about 10.8 billion people back there when I left."

Ashley was awestruck. Her jaw hung open, and she stared at Marc's shoes as if they contained some sort of answer.

"Billion?" she questioned. "I knew there were a lot more but that's crazy. People here don't really talk about Earth that much."

"It was a lot more crowded walking around compared to here, that's for sure." Marc smiled to himself. "That's why I spent most of my time in the forests or gardens. Not many people spent time there."

"Lian told me that where she was from looked a lot like the colony, but you could look up and see a blue sky, instead of the grayish-yellow one like here," Ashley added casually.

Marc stopped walking and looked at Ashley.

"Wait what? Lian isn't from here?" This was new information that Marc wasn't expecting. "I thought I was the only person that wasn't born here."

"She came when she was a teenager. The first time I saw her I think I was about halfway through school and she did one year before she started working."

"Interesting," Marc said. He also realized that meant First Minister Shen was from Earth. And he had never mentioned it. The two continued to walk through the misty warehouse.

"Yeah, she doesn't talk about it much, but sometimes she answers my questions. Probably just to shut me up."

"Why doesn't she talk about it?" Marc inquired.

"Once she mentioned that it was boring and busy all the time. If you ask me, I'd say she just likes living here much better. I'm sure you've noticed how gorgeous she is, and all the single guys around aren't afraid to tell her."

"Is that so?" Marc acted like he didn't notice but of course he had. It only took one look to see that she was extraordinary.

"And she loves the attention. I know for a fact that some people order the simplest things to be delivered just so they have an excuse to stare at her."

At least when I stared at her it was because she was dropping something off from someone else, Marc thought.

"That's really interesting. I'll have to ask her about where she's from at some point," Marc said. "So what do you do when you're not here at Nutricorps?"

"I love going to the Experience Plaza. They have some amazing experiences. My favorite one recently was The Rings of Love. It was super romantic. Basically, a girl fell for a disinterested guy but then tried to get over him but at the end the guy shrunk the rings of BZ134-4 to give her as a confession of his love." She glanced at Marc and made eye contact for the first time in a while.

"Sounds interesting," Marc commented, trying to be polite.

"Yeah, it was good but it's probably not for everyone. I'm sure you prefer adventures or mysteries or something like that."

"I'll have to check it out sometime."

Ashley and Marc made small talk for a while before he left her to assess the plants while he started mixing some chemicals for fertilizer. The fertilization system was largely automated so mixing was mostly done by calculations entered into the Garden's water system, which then pumped in the calculated percentages of nutrients and put them into solution so they could be delivered to each subsection of plants with tremendous accuracy and minimal manual work.

By the end of the day, Ashley had completed a large portion of the analyses. Marc checked through the health reports. Some of the plants looked slightly pale and off-colored. He realized the lower oxygen level may be impacting the plants' ability to take up water and nutrients. This called for an increase in water and nutrients or perhaps a decrease in nitrogen. Simple enough. He tried to focus on his work to avoid thinking about the potential oxygen catastrophe.

When Marc began to wrap things up, the door to the office space opened up and Lian walked in.

"Hey Marc," she said as she approached with her hands behind her back. Marc noted that she looked beautiful and vibrant, just like the last time he had seen her.

"Hi Lian, what can I do for you?" He was nervous talking to her. He already knew why she was there.

"Oh nothing," she said as she moved her hands in front of her to reveal a package. "I just have this Blockade set for you. A really nice one, by the way." She smiled gracefully and handed him the package.

"Wow, thank you!" Marc was happy to see Lian and to get the game.

"Don't mention it, Marc," Lian responded, laughing at his apparent excitement. "See you around." She began to turn around but Marc grabbed her arm gently.

"Lian wait!" he said in an overly aggressive shout. He toned it back. "I heard you were from Earth."

"Ashley told you?" she questioned with a slight laugh. "I'm not surprised. She has a weird way of getting people to open up and tell their life story. But yes, I'm from Earth. I came here a few decades ago though."

"Oh really? Where are you from?" Marc asked in a more relaxed tone as he leaned back in his chair, trying to act casual. Marc wasn't used to talking to gorgeous women.

"East Union," she responded.

"Oh really? I worked on greenery in a park in East Union once," Marc looked back at his memories. "Some patch of nature with a really good gelato stand."

"You know Antonio's?" Lian was shocked. Marc smiled as he found familiarity with the name. "I haven't had gelato in forever." Her tone shifted more neutral.

"Tough to find around here, I'd imagine," Marc continued. "What made you come here?"

"Sorry Marc, I'd love to keep talking but I have something really important to take care of in a couple of minutes." Lian looked at her wristband regretfully.

"Oh, I understand," Marc sighed.

"But I'm free later," she said quickly. "Would you want to meet at the game bar in about an hour? I could teach you how to play Blockade." Marc was overjoyed. He wasn't sure what type of meeting this was but he thought it would be nice to spend time with someone from back home.

"Yeah, that sounds great!" he responded.

"Great, I'll see you then," she turned to leave.

"Thanks!" Marc called as the door closed behind her.

He spent some time finishing up his calculations and digital notes for the day and headed out of the door and into the lobby. Marc waved goodbye to Ashley as he walked out the front door.

"Bye, Mr. M..." she paused, remembering their previous conversation. "Marc."

"See you tomorrow, Ashley."

As soon as he walked out into the main corridor of Government Center, he saw Greg walking proudly and sporting a wide grin. He had his usual positive outlook.

"Marc!" he yelled. "I feel like I haven't seen you in a month." He laughed, as usual. Marc laughed with him while shaking his head.

"We talked two days ago, didn't we?"

"Same difference. How was your lunch with Aran yesterday?" *I didn't see Greg yesterday*, Marc thought to himself. *How did he even know I went to lunch?*

"It was really good." Marc answered, attempting to hide his confusion. Greg picked up on it.

"Good to hear. I talked to Aran about it when I ran into him at Vertellica earlier. He seemed to think it was a productive dinner. He seemed glad you brought up your concerns and came to him with them."

"He definitely explained some things but there are still some unanswered questions we're looking into."

"Glad to hear it. I'm sure if it's Garden related you'll figure it out. After all, you're the best of the best in the world of agritechnicians." Marc felt proud yet embarrassed at the compliment. He wasn't used to flattery, especially not where he grew up. Greg continued. "Or at least in the known systems I should say. Who knows what kind of green thumbed aliens are out there, am I right?"

"Fair enough," Marc gave in to the joke and laughed.

There was silence for a minute as Marc looked down at his wrist only to realize he wasn't wearing a watch. He suddenly remembered the work he was doing earlier.

"Oh Greg," Marc began, "I hope you don't mind, but I was teaching Ashley a lot more about the Garden today. She said she wanted a little more work so I had her shadow me."

"That's fine by me, Marc. She does have an excitable ambition about her. Not to mention that she can't sit still." Marc nodded. "I have to get going though, still a couple meetings to go today."

"Sounds good. See you tomorrow." Marc walked past Greg and down the corridor.

5

arc took a magnet car to Elombe Station and made the connection towards the Game Bar. Stepping out of the car and onto the cool black marbled ground, Marc saw the reflections of the lighted signs for the local attractions.

This magnet rail only had one main stop, and that was the entrance to all of the recreation spaces. The Hexball Arena, the Game Bar, and the Experience Plaza. There were also smaller restaurants and snack shops scattered between, selling everything from veggie kebabs to fried dough to phytosteaks.

Marc passed by the multitude of activity simulation chambers. He noted people coming in and out wearing an assortment of outfits featuring things like colorful polos or flight coveralls. *I guess people prefer to dress like they're doing the real thing*, Marc thought.

The Game Bar had a runway light progression with letters made of game pieces from traditional Earth games like Pentattack and Econopoly. Marc walked into the place unfashionably early and felt out of place. As he made his way towards the imitation-wood bar, he passed several two-seat tables with built-in game boards and people moving Blockade pieces around. The players stared at the board with intense concentration and silence while groups stood around and murmured to each other.

Marc continued through the space and found himself at the dimly lit bar. It was littered with screens above a monotonous display of backlit bottles.

One of the many screens at the bar was showing a Hexball game that the colonists were playing over at the arena. Marc selected his drink of choice, something called Leto's Best Slump, from the touch screen on the bar as he continued to watch the bizarre sport.

Marc had heard of Hexball before but had never really seen it or understood the rules. The object of the game was simple; outscore the opposing teams. This part he understood because it was just like most Earth sports in that sense.

Yet it was a three-team sport, which was no kind of familiar to him.

I might as well learn how it works now, Marc thought. He sat at the bar, the man behind which wore half a beard, thick only on the left side of his face and clean shaven on the right. He brought Marc his drink and poured it into a chilled glass. It looked like foamy water but had the familiar scent of beer.

Sipping his unexpectedly viscous drink, Marc began to pick up on the rules. There were two levels of the arena, both were equal sizes, with circular openings between the two for the players to travel back and forth. The slightly lower gravity made it relatively easy for the athletes to pull themselves up or drop down quickly.

Marc noticed that there were a lot of offsides calls, which he didn't quite understand.

"Excuse me," Marc raised his hand to get the bartender's attention. "What exactly is offsides in Hexball?" The half-bearded man walked over to him.

"You don't know the rules of Hexball?" he asked. Then he gave Marc a quick look. "Oh wait, are you the agritech guy?"

"Marc," he nodded and stuck out his hand.

"Blake," the man said while meeting his grip. "Sorry for the question, everyone here grew up with the game. Offsides is pretty simple if you know what you're looking for. You see, the players are passing the ball to each other and trying to keep it from the other teams. One of the best ways to do that is to go between the two levels of the arena because you divide everyone up. Offsides is when one team has too many of their players on the same level."

"Oh, I understand," Marc said. "So it would be advantageous to make plays that force the other teams offsides."

"Exactly," Blake looked at a screen displaying a new drink order. "Let me know if you have any more questions." He walked away and went back to work.

Marc continued to watch the game. To score points, the team with the ball had to get to one of the goal tubes on three corners of the hexagonal arena, or the one in the center. Getting the ball in the tube scored your team one point.

Continuing to pick up rules one by one, except for offsides of course, Marc stared intently at the screen. Suddenly there was a close up of one of the players. It was a gorgeous and tall girl with maple hair.

"That's Lian!" Marc exclaimed to no one in particular.

She was playing! And she was good! The best, actually. She could outrun anyone, climb back and forth between the levels faster, and seemed to generally have a better strategy than the other players.

Lian scored point after point, almost single-handedly beating both of the other teams.

Marc laughed out loud and made an obvious realization. He couldn't believe that he didn't see it earlier.

Lian is genetically enhanced. Of course, Marc thought. She's younger than me, from Earth, athletically dominant, and extraordinarily attractive. How did I not make the connection before?

Marc's laughter turned into nerves as the game continued towards its end. He had been out on dates, not that this was necessarily a date, with many enhanced girls back on Earth. And it never ended well.

He remembered always going, overly excited to be with an attractive girl, trying to have a good time and connect. But they never had the same intentions. Marc was just a novelty to them. They never wanted anything more than a one-time fling or to know what life was like for someone they saw as inferior.

Marc hoped Lian wasn't the same.

Some time passed after the game had ended and Marc continued to spend time at the bar. Eventually, he saw Lian walking in, laughing with one of her teammates in their matching blue and orange jerseys. The two went separate ways as Lian headed towards Marc with her usual confident stride.

"Marc! You made it!"

"Hey Lian! So by something important earlier you meant..."

"Hexball," Lian nodded and smiled. "Hey Blake, I'll have one of these," she looked at the right half shaven man behind the bar while motioning to Marc's Slump. "Yeah, I play for the Invaders. We're doing pretty well so far this season but it's early."

"That's great! Does it help being from Earth?" she grabbed her drink from Blake and tilted her head inquisitively at Marc.

"What do you mean?"

"Well you're enhanced right?" Marc suddenly felt uncomfortable about asking the question. It had heavy implications about how he felt about her.

"I wouldn't bring that up too loud around here; some of my opponents think it's an unfair advantage and that I shouldn't be allowed to play."

"Oh, sorry," Marc said, feeling like he spoke out of turn.

"No, don't worry about it, Marc. It's not a secret. Some of the people that know enjoy playing against me for an extra challenge." She leaned in closer to Marc and lowered her voice. "And so they have an excuse when they don't win." She smiled and winked at Marc.

Marc returned the smile and paused, not knowing which direction would keep the conversation going.

"So what did you think of the game?" Lian filled the silence.

"It was really interesting. I saw a story about it back home but I'll admit, I don't think I understand all the rules yet." Marc thought back to the short documentary he

flipped to on his screen back on Earth and regretted changing the channel.

"You'll pick it up in no time. Most people here grew up
on it but I'm sure you could learn to play in a few days and
be good enough for one of the amateur leagues."

"I'll have to look into that then. Maybe you could give
me some pointers," Marc smiled at Lian and then looked at
his drink, embarrassed at his attempt to flirt.

"I'd love to!" Lian smiled and took a sip of her drink.
Marc felt the embarrassment give way to excitement. Lian
set down her glass. "Careful drinking this stuff Marc, it's
not like the stuff back on Earth."

"What do you mean?" Marc asked while picking up his
glass and examining the liquid through the light.

"It goes down easy but Slump wasn't made for casual
drinking. It was originally made as a drinkable anesthetic.
They've toned it down since then but it's still strong."

"You're kidding!" Marc's jaw dropped. "It tastes so
light!"

"Yeah it'll sneak up on you, especially since you're not
used to it."

"Thanks for the tip."

"Come on," Lian grabbed Marc's hand. "I want to show
you something." Marc was careful to grab his drink in his
other hand while Lian led him away from the bar.

"Where are we going?" Marc asked while trying to match Lian's long strides.

"Right here." She stopped at one of the two-seat tables and gestured for Marc to sit down. "Want to play Blockade?"

Marc nodded as he took his seat and placed his drink down on the table, his hand wet from the condensation on the glass.

"It's a pretty simple game," she started to explain as she pulled open a sliding drawer on the side of the table. She removed black and orange pieces and began setting them on the seven by seven square grid. "Blockade was created here so I figured you wouldn't know it. Though you have been here for a while now, but I'm sure you've been busy. It's a little different than most games because each person has a different win condition. Do you want to be the Blockade or the Smuggler?" Lian looked up from the board and met Marc's eyes with a subtle smile.

"Is one easier than the other?"

"A lot of people think being the Smuggler is easier but you usually play one game as each, and sometimes a third if both players win one game." Lian explained. "Of course, there are quicker tournaments where you only play as one or the other."

"Let me start off as the Smuggler then," Marc gave a slight laugh.

"So then you're going to be the black pieces in the middle of the board," Lian motioned to five pieces set up in the center of the grid in a plus formation, with one taller spacecraft in the middle, surrounded by four smaller vehicles.

"Why do I have less pieces than you?" Marc furrowed his brow with confusion.

"The Smuggler has five pieces, the smaller ones are called Distractors and the big one is called the Runner. Since I'm the Blockade, I have twelve Blockers. I promise it's fair," Lian laughed. "Everything make sense so far?" Marc studied the Blockers. They were arranged in the three middle spaces on each edge of the grid, surrounding Marc's Runner and Distractors.

"We'll see, I guess."

"So all of the pieces move the same way," Lian continued. "They can move X or Y direction, as many spaces as you want, but can't move into or pass through other pieces."

"Simple enough," Marc said. "How do you win?"

"So you, since you're the Smuggler, want to win by moving the Runner to one of the corner spaces called Exits." Marc noticed the corner spaces were white, while the rest of the board was a black and orange checker pattern, except for the middle space, which was also white.

"And how do you win?"

"I win by capturing your Runner," Lian seemed to be finished with her explanation. She looked at Marc and smiled. "Ready to play?"

"Wait, how do you capture my pieces?"

"Oh right! We can both capture each other's pieces, to do that you need to surround them on two opposing sides or by making it unable to move by pinning it against the edge of the board. Once you do, you can remove it from the game. The Runner is the only piece that can move into the Exits and I can only capture the Runner by surrounding it on all four sides." Now Lian was finished.

Marc thought to himself for a moment, processing the rules. The game seemed simple in the rules but no doubt there was an immense amount of hidden strategy involved.

"Ready to play now? I didn't forget any rules this time," Lian smiled looking at Marc.

"Sure, let's do it." Marc reached out to move one of his Distractors but Lian interrupted.

"Oh sorry, Marc. The Blockade always moves first." She proceeded to reach out a graceful hand and moved one of her Blockers towards one of Marc's Distractors. Marc followed with a move of his own. He attempted to move his pieces all towards one side as Lian countered each and every action. He attempted to slide his Runner out but Lian predicted the move with ease. Soon she had ended the game by moving a fourth Blocker to surround the Runner.

"Not bad, Marc," Lian said while maintaining her smile. She clearly enjoyed winning.

"Is it usually that short of a game?" Marc asked while trying to gauge the sincerity of Lian's comment.

"Not usually, no," she admitted. "But it wasn't fast because you were bad. It was more of the opposite. You picked up on some basic strategy right away and your decision making was quicker than most people I play against."

"So what you're saying is that I should take my time and consider my moves more?" Marc laughed and Lian joined him.

"No, I'm serious. With a little practice, you could be a serious competitor."

"Maybe I'll stick with it then. Are people always here to play?" he asked.

"For the most part. I would say you could probably find someone looking for a game at least six out of seven days you come here. And there are obviously tournaments that bring out the more competitive players." Lian began grabbing the pieces and placing them back into the side drawer.

"Is there some kind of kids league I could join?" Marc jested. "I might have a shot with them." Lian burst into laughter.

"No, no, Marc. There's no kids league that would let you join," Lian said while fighting back more laughter. "There is a Blockade app you can use on your digipad or any of your displays if you want some more practice against the AI."

"Oh good to know," Marc continued to smile.

"I'm glad you're willing to learn, I'm always looking for a new challenger."

"Who's the best player here then?" Marc asked while looking around the bar.

"Don't look too far," Lian raised one eyebrow to go with her smile. "I'm right here."

Marc laughed again. He could already tell Lian was smart but didn't know that she would be the best one around. *I guess she was enhanced back on Earth*, he reminded himself.

"So you're the reigning Blockade champion these days?" Marc tried to match her raised eyebrow without success. Lian noticed the effort and chuckled.

"As of right now, yes. I won last month's tournament and no one has been able to beat me since."

"Well maybe your Earth brain has some advantages," Marc joked.

"Maybe."

Marc suddenly thought back to his previous night's conversation with First Minister Shen, Lian's father. He thought about the lower oxygen concentration and its effect on the people.

"Hey Lian, can I ask you something?"

"Sure Marc, what's up?"

"I was talking to Aran yesterday," he began. "And he said that you spread a rumor about him the other day." He hesitated to bring up what was really on his mind.

"Yes," she smiled just thinking about it. "I did."

"Do you mind if I ask why?"

"Not at all, Marc. I've done it a few times. My poor father thinks that I do it just to mess with him, but it's more complex than he realizes," she said.

"Enlighten me."

"Well, what I do is put doubt into the minds of the people in the colony. Doubts about whether the First Minister is looking out for their best interests."

"What's the point of that?" Marc asked.

"The point is that I know he can handle it, and he will go out and very publicly say that he is fighting for the rights of the people in the colony. And that he wants what's best for them and their futures." Lian finished speaking and examined Marc's face.

"So you do it," Marc worked through the information. "Not to make people doubt him, but to actually reinforce why he is a great leader?"

"Exactly, Marc." Lian was glad he understood. "Most people don't get it, but every time I spread a rumor like this, their support for him grows and it solidifies his place as the leader of the Makan Colony. Not that it was ever really in question by the general public."

"Wow," Marc smiled. "That's actually genius." Lian wasn't a bad daughter. She was actually the opposite.

"Thank you, I try my best." She smiled back at him.

"Can I ask you something else?"

"Of course, Marc."

"Do you know anything about the oxygen percentage in the colony and how it compares to back on Earth?"

"I don't really know anything about it. Why do you ask?" Lian tilted her head to the side.

"Well," Marc became uncomfortable as he forced himself to elaborate. "The oxygen back on Earth was constantly sitting at 21 percent in the atmosphere. And here it's supposed to be 19 percent. But I did an experiment in the Garden and I found out that in the colony it sits at about 17.4 percent."

Lian looked at Marc, letting the information sink in. She was expressionless for a moment, but then displayed confusion. Finally she decided to speak.

"Sorry Marc, I don't really know that much about air science. Is that a big difference?"

"That's what I'm trying to figure out," Marc responded. "And I think it might cause people here to have difficulty fully developing their brains. But I'm not positive about that."

"Have you told anyone about the difference?" Lian's eyes lit up with surprise. "Surely that can be fixed, right?"

"I told Greg at first. He dismissed the difference as being meaningless. To him the difference might as well not exist. Then I told Aran and he's looking into it with Vertellica, but I haven't heard anything back yet."

"That's so strange," Lian said. "So then it's not actually having an effect? Was your experiment accurate?"

"Yes, I'm positive my experiment was accurate because I did that to test if the Garden's oxygen probes were functioning correctly. I haven't been here long enough to know if there is a noticeable effect."

"So what are you going to do?" Lian asked.

"I guess I'm going to wait and see if Vertellica knows anything about it. I'm just worried that it could have to do with the people that have died unexpectedly over the last year." Marc looked down at the table. He was talking more to himself now than Lian. He wanted to try to think things through again.

"If my father and Vertellica know about it then I guess everything is somewhat under control? Or at least it will be soon?" Lian looked to Marc for reassurance. She didn't find any.

"I'm not sure. Something about the whole situation just rubs me the wrong way," Marc said as he looked back at Lian.

"Do you have any control over the oxygen because of your work at Nutricorps?" Lian probed further.

"It seems like I should, but I actually don't. The Garden has the same air composition as the rest of the colony, excluding the increased humidity."

"You might want to look into Vertellica," Lian added. "It seems like something they would control."

"You're probably right," Marc said. "I guess right now all I can do is observe and see if there really is anything else going on."

"Whatever you think is right, Marc," Lian said. "Just make sure you're careful. Vertellica has a tendency to hide information from the public. I'm sure you remember that from Earth but it's worse here."

"I know what you mean. Thanks, Lian," Marc said. "It's been good to get this off my chest and talk to someone about it."

There was a sudden faint beeping sound. Lian looked down at a wristband on her arm.

"Oh sorry, Marc!" she said, surprised. "I have to go. My team celebration just started and I'm running late."

"Oh," Marc responded. "I understand. You seem to enjoy winning so I'd hate to keep you from celebrating that." He smiled and Lian began to stand up.

"This was fun," Lian smiled back at Marc. "We should do it again."

"I would enjoy that."

And with that, Lian walked away at a brisk pace, again checking her wristband and then breaking into a light jog. He remained seated for a moment to finish his drink. He then headed home for the evening.

6

The next day, Lian came walking through the door to the Nutricorps office space.

"Another delivery?" Marc joked. Lian didn't smile back. She seemed strangely serious. Almost worried in a way.

"Is everything okay?" Marc asked when she stopped.

"I thought a lot about what you told me yesterday, about oxygen levels here and." She paused again, and snapped a look at the surrounding area, checking for eavesdroppers. "I think I found something you might want to see."

Something about her tone worried Marc. She looked like she had seen murder. But he had to ask.

"What is it?"

"Come with me." Lian grabbed Marc's arm and lifted him out of his seat. He knew he had no choice but to follow.

Lian escorted Marc away from his desk and out into the lobby.

"I'll be back in a bit, Ashley," Marc called out as they walked by. Ashley looked at Lian's hand still holding Marc's arm and then nodded without a smile. Lian's grip tightened as they continued out the Nutricorps doors. It was around midday so there were plenty of people walking around in Government Center. Everyone seemed to be on a meal break.

Lian escorted Marc to the left, across the space under the grayish yellow sky and towards some of the other facility doors. She continued without words and with a fierce focus in her eyes. Marc stayed quiet in anticipation of what the next few moments might bring.

After passing through a small crowd and walking a short distance, Lian stopped and looked up. Marc followed her eyes to the sign above the black tinted glass double doors. *Vertellica.*

"What are we doing here?" Marc asked. "Getting some equipment for the Garden?" Marc knew the answer to his second question was negative.

"If anyone asks, I'm giving you a tour," Lian turned and lowered her gaze to meet Marc's eyes.

"*Are* you giving me a tour?" Marc asked with confusion, grasping for any form of clarification.

"Something like that." Lian started walking in the Vertellica doors and Marc followed half a step behind. They passed into a lobby similar to the one at Nutricorps, with a reception desk close to the back wall and a secured door to its side. There was no receptionist.

Lian continued walking up to the security door. Marc thought about asking what the plan was but decided silence was the best action.

The door beeped and slid open once Lian got close enough.

"Vertellica has less security than Nutricorps? Who would've thought," Marc decided to break the silence.

"No it has more, Marc." Lian responded and shot a look at Marc as if to say *stop talking*.

They passed through the door and continued through office spaces similar to Marc's, all of which seemed to be empty at the moment. They walked down a hallway between two labs. Inside one of the labs were three scientists gowned up to the maximum biosafety level. They seemed to be crowded around some kind of black metallic cube. Lian paid no attention but Marc's curiosity grew.

After continuing through the labyrinth of office spaces, labs, and common rooms, Lian halted at what appeared to be a cleaning closet. No markings were on the door and it had a simple lock requiring a passcode. Most of the doors in the colony were biometrically secured so seeing a small screen with digital numbers was strangely low tech.

Lian used her hand to balance herself against the door as she bent over to type in some numbers. Marc noted the numbers she typed from the corner of his eye.

5-1-4-1-3.

"Don't tell my father," Lian said.

"About what?" Marc asked.

"That I just used his access code." Marc glanced at her confused.

The door made a light clicking sound and then slid open, revealing a somewhat large room walled with some kind of blinking black machines. At the center of the back wall sat a desk with one screen on its surface and many on the wall behind it.

"What is this room?" Marc asked Lian after they passed into the room. The door slid shut quietly behind them. Lian made her way to the desk and then turned to Marc.

"This is Vertellica's central information hub. It houses all the data and recorded information from the colony, and a lot of their private data from Earth. It can usually be accessed on their employee computers, but the desk screen in this room has access to some higher security information."

Marc tried to gather his thoughts while studying the room and feeling the breeze of the many cooling fans around him.

"So what are we doing here?" He finally asked.

"I was thinking about what you said last night. You know, about the potential negative effects of lower oxygen levels. It got me thinking, so I came here. Luckily I found a lonely scientist working late at night and flirted with him until he let me in to make a delivery." She said the last bit with air quotes. Lian began typing on the desk screen, and the screens against the wall turned on in response.

"So did you find anything about it?" Marc asked. Lian nodded and continued to work on the screen. Her long, graceful fingers worked over the device quickly.

"This is a summary of the data from the studies that Vertellica conducted. Take a look for yourself." Lian stepped to the side and away from the screen after tapping one more time. The wall screens lit up, each with different data sets.

Marc moved a step closer, squinting to examine the screens one by one. Scrolling through, he read experiment write-ups that referenced human physiological balance. He stared at element concentration by tissue type across multiple samples. The data included a summary on pH and metabolism.

> Mean physiological pH of Makan Colony
> humans is 6.9 compared to a reference
> Earth population pH of 7.4. Adjusting
> colony air composition has a signif-
> icant impact on bodily pH, leading to
> more acidic physiological environ-
> ments. Notable anatomic effects are
> exhibited by slightly enlarged kid-
> neys, liver, and lungs while general
> metabolism is decreased.

Marc read back over the information. He hadn't noticed any abnormal looking people so the development of larger organs wasn't severe enough to be noticeable. He expected the decreased metabolism based on the size of meals he had seen in the colony and based on the size of the Garden. He continued to read the research summaries Lian brought to his attention.

> Human health minimally affected when
> reducing atmospheric Oxygen by 2%
> over the course of several weeks.
> Side effects include cough, brief
> nausea, and confusion. Following

Marc thought back to his trip to the Makan Colony. He now understood why he hadn't noticed any of the effects of the lower oxygen availability. The shuttle that brought him here had gradually adjusted its air composition. He continued reading.

One after another, Marc read through the screens. Many had similar conclusions. Rapid changes in oxygen levels have a negative effect on mental development, though a slower change may have less of an impact.

"This is exactly what I expected," Marc whispered. He began tapping on the screens rapidly and brought up a new study. Lian looked over Marc's shoulder for more answers.

```
Reduction in Oxygen level is shown
to have negative effects on health
that increase with age. Symptoms in-
clude lack of coordination, confu-
sion, and altered breathing rate.
Symptoms have been commonly identi-
fied in patients over the age of 70.
6 deaths due to hypoxia have been
observed.
```

"This study was updated this week. The woman that died in Elombe Station must've been the sixth." Marc's worried eyes looked at Lian. He found similar worry in her gaze.

"Over the age of 70?" Lian said. Marc knew what she was thinking. "My father could be slowly dying and no one even knows."

Marc nodded without a verbal response.

"We have to do something. Or tell someone," Lian turned around and began to pace. "Before it's too late."

"We can tell Aran," Marc reassured her. "And he should be able to make some changes."

"I don't know how they've been able to keep this a secret for so long," Lian responded, barely listening to Marc.

"Vertellica is letting people die because of the low oxygen levels and they're not doing anything to change it. I don't understand why they would…" Marc's voice trailed off into thoughtful silence.

"Vertellica controls everything, maybe even my father." Lian stepped up to the desk screen and began tapping again. Pretty soon she had finished and she pulled up a new file on the screens.

"I've heard him shouting with Vertellica people about Project Magellan," she continued to make the file visible. "Maybe that can tell us about Vertellica's plan."

Lian looked back at Marc, her eyes were wide and staring directly into Marc's. Marc stared back intently, still processing all of this new information.

"But what…" Marc was interrupted by three loud knocks against the metal door.

"Who's in there?" An unknown voice called through the door. Marc and Lian stood silently. Then they heard more footsteps approaching.

"How are we going to get out of here?" Marc whispered to Lian.

Then suddenly the door slid open and three men walked into the room. All dressed in green uniforms, each with stunners on their hips.

WOSE security guards. Marc recognized their attire and realized that he was in for some trouble.

"You're going to have to come with us," the first guard to enter the room spoke monotonously. He approached Marc, grabbed him by the shoulders and escorted him out of the room. One of the other guards did the same to Lian. Neither Marc nor Lian said a single word all the while they were being taken away.

Marc was left to contemplate the findings in his own mind as they continued out of the Vertellica facility and towards the Government Center magnet rail.

7

The magnet car stopped. The door slid open and the security guards nudged Marc and Lian into the large room. A familiar crystal chandelier hung from the ceiling.

The guards brought them to First Minister Shen's residence. They stopped walking once they reached the chandelier. The First Minister walked into the room wearing a sleek black suit with textured lapels. Beside him was the WOSE security commissioner. The two gave each other a nod of understanding.

"On me," the commissioner said to the guards and he led them back out to the magnet car. Marc and Lian were now alone with First Minister Shen.

"So why don't you tell me what you two were doing looking at Vertellica's secure database?" he looked at Marc, then to Lian, and back at Marc.

Marc opened his mouth to answer but Lian spoke over him.

"I was just showing Marc how to access data files that he might need for his agritech optimizations. And then we found something else…" She was cut off.

"Lian, go to the library and wait for me there. I'm going to talk to Marc alone for a minute." She hesitated and looked at Marc, then walked away obediently at the command of her father. Aran threw his arm around Marc's back and patted him on the shoulder. "Come with me, Marc."

The two walked into a neighboring room and First Minister Shen pressed on the wall to close the door behind them.

Marc looked around the room. There was a single table in the middle, similar to the ones at the Game Bar. It had the seven-by-seven gridded board on top and drawers on the side to hold the pieces. In the corner of the room was a bureau with a pot on it. A small mass of yellow and purple lined the inside.

"So why'd you do it, Marc?" First Minister Shen broke the silence as Marc turned back to face him. "Vertellica is going to expect some kind of punishment. Hopefully I can talk them down to something small." His frustration was evident.

"I just wanted some more information," Marc answered simply.

"You shouldn't have broken into Vertellica. Had you asked, I would've gladly helped you to see whatever data systems you wanted." His face showed genuine confusion.

"I think I figured out why people are dying," Marc said, measuring the effect of his words.

"Did you?" the First Minister asked. "Anything to do with the Garden?"

"No," came Marc's quick response. "It's the low oxygen level."

"Just as you suspected, then. Tell me, Marc, what all did you read to lead you to that conclusion?"

"I read general studies about initial oxygen levels and the negative impacts on mental development…"

"Those are old studies," the First Minister interrupted. "More recent ones have come out that show people develop normally after a brief adjustment period. But continue."

"Well I read about the lowered physiological pH and the harmful effects of low oxygen levels on the older population."

First Minister Shen made no move to interrupt Marc's speech so he proceeded.

"The Vertellica files specifically linked the low oxygen level to the deaths of six people in the colony," Marc said explicitly.

The First Minister's eyebrows narrowed as he looked away from Marc. He made no comment as he thought.

"Aran," Marc said as the aged man met Marc's eyes. "I'm saying this as a friend. The low oxygen levels put you at risk. Your health could be gradually declining with no obvious symptoms. Lian is worried about you." This last statement hit the First Minister hard. His face showed concern mixed with sadness.

"Worrying Lian is the last thing I want," he finally said. He opened his mouth again but then hesitated.

"There has to be some way to set things back to normal." Marc looked at First Minister Shen with hope. He was quiet, thinking about his daughter. Marc thought about the other information Lian had mentioned.

"What's Project Magellan?" Marc asked. "Lian thought that might be related."

First Minister Shen took a moment to gather himself and his thoughts.

"It is related," he admitted. "I can fill you in on more of the details soon."

"What is it?"

"Let's wait and see what Vertellica's plan is for you. Then we can get into it. They've been wanting me to get you to work for them for some time now, but I told them you had to focus on stabilizing the food supply for now." First Minister Shen seemed reluctant to share any more details.

"So I'll learn more from Vertellica?"

"Yes, I'm sure they'll fill you in shortly." The First Minister spoke with subtle annoyance towards Vertellica.

"Why would Vertellica knowingly endanger and impair the entire colony population?" Marc asked.

"You don't understand the big picture, Marc." First Minister Shen's voice became calm and measured.

"Then explain it to me. Maybe go slow just in case the oxygen deficiency is slowing my brain." Marc's response came off aggressively and he looked at the First Minister apologetically.

"Vertellica believes they know better than everyone else. 'Sometimes the incorrectly perceived wisdom of the greater population gets in the way of progress being made for their own benefit.'" First Minister Shen said as if quoting someone. Marc listened as he took a few steps towards one of the corners of the room.

"But can't you outrank them or tell them to make changes? You're the First Minister." Marc had reached the bureau in the corner and put one of his hands in the pot. He brushed his hands through the small plant and noted the star shape of the leaves. *Rafflesia aerobia*, Marc recognized the beautiful growth.

First Minister Shen watched Marc closely in the corner while he continued speaking, "Unfortunately, Vertellica has a lot of power here, maybe even more than myself," he said begrudgingly.

Marc removed his hand and turned back towards the First Minister. He took a few steps back towards the center of the room.

"What kind of progress are they trying to make? Is there some kind of hidden benefit that I haven't seen yet?" Marc asked poignant questions.

"Vertellica has the colony's best interest in mind, or so they think," First Minister Shen said cryptically. "You just have to trust me on that for now and I can fill you in on more details at a later date. It's not all under my control."

"Let me ask you one more thing, just so I understand better," said Marc.

The First Minister nodded.

"Why lower the oxygen concentration? Why not just engineer people to live in this environment during standard IVF procedures?"

"Are you familiar with epigenetics, Marc?" First Minister Shen showed no surprise at Marc's question.

"I've heard the term," Marc responded.

"Epigenetics is essentially the study of how environmental factors influence gene expression. You see, Vertellica believes it's safer for unmodified people to be constantly exposed to a specific environmental stimulus, in this case, lower oxygen levels," the First Minister continued. "Genetically engineering people is too…" he paused to think of the word. "Polarizing. What we think might be the best modifications now could result in greater health risks later on. And it is difficult to understand the potential effects of passing those engineered genes on to future generations."

Marc looked at him with understanding. "So rather than engineer people, Vertellica keeps people natural with their evolutionary ability to adapt slowly over time," Marc stated. "Because that's safer?"

"Exactly right, Marc," First Minister Shen began to explain further. "That's the way Vertellica sees it anyways. The difference between genetically modifying the people of the Makan Colony and subjecting them to epigenetic pressures is that it allows for adaptation."

"So you're saying that over time people will get used to the oxygen deprivation?" Marc asked in disbelief.

"It's certainly possible. It probably already happened in the younger generations," First Minister Shen answered. "That's what Vertellica thinks and why things haven't changed. But if that's causing people to die like you say…" he trailed off.

"It seems like they already have the evidence they need to change it," Marc said. "Can you put some extra pressure on them?"

"I'll do what I can, Marc." the First Minister responded. "You know I want what's best for everyone."

"Thank you, Aran," Marc showed some relief.

"But keep in mind, Marc. Vertellica and I don't agree on everything. And there's certainly some things that are out of my control. Hopefully we have the opportunity to guide the colony towards its best possible future. But for now, Vertellica insisted that I have security escort you home." Marc looked over at the colorful plant in the corner.

"Why have you never mentioned that you're from Earth?"

"Two reasons, Marc." The First Minister paused and looked at him with intelligent eyes. "The first is that I came here so long ago, that I barely think about that life and that helps me to make decisions for what's best for everyone in the Makan Colony. The second is your background. I know you grew up around the enhanced and it was difficult being different. I wanted you to accept me as a friend, not as someone you thought looked down on you."

Marc nodded, taking time to think through the First Minister's answers.

"Have a good night, Marc." First Minister Shen walked towards the metal door and it slid open. A security guard

appeared in the room and escorted him back to his residence in silence.

8

At a nod from the security guard, Marc placed his hand on the door to his apartment. It quickly slid open and he stepped in. The guard remained outside as the door slid closed behind Marc.

The apartment felt cold as he walked through the kitchen. He noticed his rainbow sequoia. It had grown ever so slightly since he last checked on it. Marc found a cup in his cabinet and filled it with water, which he then poured around the base of the tiny tree sprout.

He looked at the mug next to the sequoia. There was no sign of growth. The *Rafflesia aerobia* wasn't growing. *Nothing surprising there*, Marc thought.

He had a sudden realization. He thought back to his recent time spent with First Minister Shen. He remembered running his hands through the yellow and purple groundcover growing in the pot on the bureau. *Why would it grow there but not here?* The answer was obvious to him.

Marc sat down at the kitchen counter and let the thought sink in. His head filled with anger and despair. He never expected to be coming into such a broken system. Everything back on Earth talked about how revolutionary the Makan Colony was and how perfectly efficient everything seemed.

Some time passed as Marc's thoughts raced. It seemed like minutes had gone by when he heard a knocking at the door. Marc looked to the nearest screen to see the time. It was almost night time.

He walked to the door and it opened to reveal the same guard that had escorted Marc home. *Has he been here the whole time?* Marc asked himself.

"First Minister Shen requested that I bring you to a meeting at the WOSE office," the guard said without emotion. He took a step back and held his arm out gesturing for Marc to leave his apartment. Marc obeyed, knowing he didn't have a choice. He had been to the WOSE office, but only once for a meeting.

"Let's go then," Marc responded. The two began their walk back to the magnet rail. When the two got into the car, Marc decided to make conversation.

"Have you lived in the colony your whole life?"

"Yes, I was born here," the guard responded briefly.

"So do you work specifically for the First Minister or for Vertellica or what?" Marc continued his survey. The magnet car was moving back towards Elombe Station.

"I work for WOSE." He wasn't much of a talker. Marc kept silent for a minute, then thought of another question.

"How many people in the colony work for WOSE?"

"Stop asking questions, I'm not supposed to talk much while I'm working," The guard looked at Marc, then back at the glass in the front of the car. They pulled into Elombe Station and switched tracks.

Marc's curiosity wasn't satisfied. He asked another question.

"Has anyone ever left the colony to go back to Earth?"

"Once or twice, now stop asking questions." Marc looked at the large, broad-shouldered man, studying him like he did his plants.

"A guy built like you must play hexball," he commented. "Who's your team?" The guard looked at Marc out of the corner of his eyes. Then he slowly smiled.

"Warriors," he admitted. "Do you play?"

"No, I'm afraid I haven't had the chance yet."

"You should!" the guard said enthusiastically. "It's a great workout. And nothing feels better than winning."

"Do you ever play the Invaders?" Marc asked, remembering Lian's team name. The guard's passion faded to annoyance.

"Yeah."

"Are they good?" Marc asked.

"It depends how you look at it," the guard began, now talking with extravagant hand movements. "A lot of people think that their team is unfair, and that they shouldn't be allowed in the main league. They have certain advantages that no other team can have."

"Like Lian?"

"She's enhanced! Playing against the rest of us normal people. Does that seem fair to you?"

"I don't know," Marc answered. "But I'd love to be on the team that beats her and proves that being enhanced doesn't make them better than us." It was a mindset Marc had developed when growing up around exclusively enhanced people.

"Now you're talking," the guard's smile expanded. "I'll tell you what. Once all this business with Vertellica and the First Minister is cleared up, you should find me in the Hexball Arena sometime."

"I'll do that," Marc said, enjoying the idea of getting more familiar with the strange sport.

They arrived at Government Center.

"Let's go," the guard said as he got out of the car. Marc followed as the guard led him down the corridor. There were few people walking around, most were either home or at the recreation center at this point. They walked down past Leto's Best, past the Waste Management Department, past Nutricorps, and to the end of the hall to the WOSE office.

The glass doors with the WOSE logo on them parted as they walked up. Marc and the guard passed through the lobby, by a seating area and walked through two more sliding doors into a large room.

The room was full of people seated at a large circular table. One open chair remained. The guard stopped at the entrance to the room. It was a meeting for the Makan Colony's Advisory Council. Marc had only ever attended one meeting before, and that was to fill in for Greg when couldn't make it to give a work update about Nutricorps.

"Marc! Good to see you!" Greg was seated next to the empty chair. "I saved you a seat." He motioned for Marc to walk over and sit next to him.

"Oh hi, Greg," Marc responded. Marc made his way over to the empty seat and realized that his seat was the only one without a name displayed in front of it.

"I'm glad you're here, Marc." Another familiar voice rang out. Marc picked his head up as he pulled his chair back to sit down. First Minister Shen sat opposite Marc. He began to move onto business. "Great to see you all here. This should be a short meeting just for general updates. Let's start with the recreation center. Anyone have any important updates regarding business there?"

A bespectacled man with a handlebar mustache began to speak.

"Tomorrow is our monthly Blockade tournament." Marc read the man's display to see that he was the Council member representing the Game Bar. "We expect a similar turnout to last month, and we're offering a special drink deal in partnership with Leto's for the night to try to attract some more spectators."

There was a short silence where no one spoke as everyone waited to hear more about the affairs of the recreation center. A man broke the silence. His face sported a thick beard, only on the right side. His left was clean shaven. The opposite side of the man who served Marc his drink at the Game Bar. *He must be Blake's*, Marc paused to think of the word, *twin*. Twins were exceedingly rare since the universal adoption of IVF.

"Hi, I'm filling in for the Experience Plaza. I was told to come and update everyone that our newest experience should be arriving from Earth within the next week. It's called Space Viking. It's supposed to be an action science fiction experience about a ship of men and women that begin to raid planet settlements in the hopes to create a new coalition of colonies."

"Good to hear, Jake," the First Minister responded. "Anything else?"

A few of the other Council members shook their heads.

"Business as usual," someone said.

"Okay great, moving on then," First Minister Shen kept the meeting moving. "Let's go to the Department of Expansion. Any updates on the new construction?"

"Yes, we've made some major progress recently," a burly man began speaking in a raspy voice. "The new residential space is almost complete. We also finished the surface lab earlier this week, but that wasn't much work. Except for the airlock installation."

"The surface lab is ready for use?" First Minister Shen asked with his eyebrows raised.

"Yes, it's all set," the burly man responded, giving a thumbs up.

"Fantastic. That's great news." First Minister Shen tapped on the table, causing the natural pattern to fade and a screen to appear in front of him. He appeared to be taking some notes. "Okay then, let's move on to Nutricorps. What do you have for us, Greg?" Greg stood up before speaking.

"Everything is going great, everything in the Garden seems healthy. That's all thanks to Marc here," he patted

Marc on the shoulder. "We've been optimizing everything to use resources more efficiently." Greg took his seat.

"Thank you, Greg," the First Minister continued to moderate. "For those of you that don't know, Marc Morrison, sitting next to Greg, is the newest Nutricorps employee and agritech expert. We brought him in from Earth a little over a year ago because we were told he's the best. You might not have seen him around; he's been working day and night to fix the mess that was left after the unexpected passing of the previous agritech expert."

First Minister Shen was looking around and speaking to everyone, though most eyes were directed at Marc. Marc held a hand up and gave a gentle smile to acknowledge everyone. The eyes soon shifted back to the speaker.

"And unfortunately, I have a bad piece of news for all of you, which is not to leave the Council. Marc is curious by nature, which is of course what makes him excellent at his job. However, earlier today, around lunch time, Marc accessed Vertellica's central information hub without permission." All eyes were again on Marc, some heads shaking, some eyebrows narrowed with confusion. Greg showed no surprise. *He must've been told already*, Marc thought.

"Security found him looking at data sets from past experiments relevant to the colony's founding and air composition. Of course, this information is related to his work and he is still learning the differences between our rules and those back on Earth," First Minister Shen gave Marc some subtle support to soften the judgement. "I have worked with the folks at Vertellica to decide an appropriate punishment, since they are the ones affected by Marc's misguided actions." The council members nodded in understanding.

Marc felt uncomfortable.

"Rishad, would you care to take it from here?" First Minister Shen said with a subtle eye roll that only Marc seemed to notice. The two didn't exactly get along but tried to act professional around others.

"Absolutely. Rishad Bansri," a man with slicked back black hair, waved as an introduction to Marc. He was short in stature and had a perfectly clean-shaven face. "You see Marc, we've discussed this event with the First Minister and with Greg. And we've decided on a suitable retribution."

"What is it?" Marc asked?

"We're not going to charge you with anything, you won't be confined to your apartment for the foreseeable future, and you definitely won't be sent back to Earth. But you will have to atone for your actions by helping us with research." Rishad gave a slight grin.

"What kind of research?" Marc was both curious and nervous. *What could they possibly want me to do?*

"Seeing as you're so interested in the air composition and the effect it has on life; we're going to give you the opportunity to do research of great importance to the health of the colony. Also, something that relates to your fascination with agritech." He spoke a lot without saying much.

"Could you be more specific?" Marc asked.

"We'll talk about it more later on," Rishad responded. "We just wanted to inform everyone on the Council of the recent events and let them know that everything is being handled appropriately. We would hate to keep anyone in the dark."

"But for now, let's just continue with the meeting," First Minister Shen began speaking again. "Let's move on to the Fabrication Corporation. How are you doing on materials?"

"We're doing pretty well," a red-haired woman began speaking. "We have everything we need for now, we're really ramping up the furniture production for the new residential zone."

"Thanks for the update. How has that been impacting mining operations?" The First Minister looked across the table for an answer.

"We're doing well. One of the bots has been temperamental lately but we're taking care of it. We still have two running normal enough."

"Good to hear. Does anyone else have any important updates that we haven't yet addressed?" First Minister Shen asked the group.

There was a brief silence filled with people looking back and forth at each other. No one had anything to say.

"Great, this will be a short meeting then. We'll meet at the same time as always next week. Thank you all for coming." People began to push back in their chairs and stand up. Marc started to do the same. First Minister Shen noticed this. "Marc, hold on a moment. You, Greg, and the Vertellica reps need to stick around."

Everyone else continued to get up and leave. The remaining few of them sat in silence for a minute while the rest made their way out the doors. There were seven of them left once everyone had gone. First Minister Shen, Marc, Greg, Rishad, and three other Vertellica representatives.

Marc made note of the name plates for the three he had not yet been introduced to. There was a brunette with her hair in a ponytail and wearing squared spectacles. Another had thick dark hair and seemed to have a cheery disposition. The third man, John, was bald and even tempered. All three wore similar pastel orange button down shirts with the Vertellica logo adorned on the left breast pocket. Rishad wore the same shirt, yet had a brown blazer over top.

"So, Rishad," First Minister Shen began. "Would you like to explain your research project to Marc and Greg?"

"Of course! I think it has the potential to be a very valuable project. It's actually the entire reason we built a new lab on the planet's surface. The goal is to create healthy plant life on the surface." He finished speaking so casually, as if this was going to be an easy project. Greg was first to respond.

"How the hell are we supposed to do that?" He didn't show his usual good-humored self. He was noticeably perplexed.

"We have every reason to believe it's possible with the technology and expertise we have available to us," Rishad responded, nodding towards Marc.

"What kind of technology do you expect to be able to help?" Marc decided to jump in now. "Most plants have very specific growth requirements and they've evolved to fit Earth's environment over the course of millions and millions of years."

"We're very aware of evolution, Marc," Rishad said while laughing. "Don't forget that Vertellica has led most scientific advancements in the colony and on Earth for two centuries."

"Fair enough, but plants are difficult to control. They can grow in harsh environments but keep in mind that they still need oxygen levels sufficient enough to undergo normal respiration processes. What's your plan?" Marc asked. The bald Vertellica representative cleared his throat.

"Let me introduce myself," he said. "And then I may be able to help explain some of the project since I'll be working with you."

Marc nodded in response.

"I'm John Riley, and I'm Vertellica's head of genetics in Makan. The plan is that we put our heads together and engineer some new strains of existing plants, that way they may be able to survive the harsh surface environment."

"You think that such significant changes can be made to alter the way the plants metabolize?" Marc asked rhetorically.

"That's what we want to find out," John decided to respond.

"Why would we do that? I thought we were trying to find new habitable planets to spread to, not stay on this one," Marc looked back to First Minister Shen for answers.

"A good point," the First Minister began speaking again. "The problem is, we haven't found any options. And it's not for a lack of trying. WOSE back on Earth has been researching every planet and solar system within a traversable range since the colony was established. Nothing came up that was more suitable than our very own surface."

"And so the goal now is…" Marc waited for someone to finish his sentence.

"To terraform," Rishad added. "And this is the first of many steps to make it possible."

Marc sat in silence for some time while thinking through the new information. Greg spoke next.

"So what's the timeline looking like?" he asked. "It'll take at least a couple centuries to make the air breathable.

And that's if the engineering works like it's planned. Unless we grow some kind of space gills."

Greg was back to his good-humored self and everyone responded with a light chuckle.

"Our calculations and preliminary studies indicate that it could be much sooner than that," the brunette woman decided to jump in. "Assuming we're successful with our surface experiments."

"We can discuss everything further in the next couple of days," Rishad added as he turned to Marc. "We just wanted to introduce you to the project. You and John can meet tomorrow to discuss more specifics."

"And this project is called…" Marc waited for an answer.

"Project T," John answered. Marc looked at the First Minister and cocked his head. He expected a different name.

"Looks like that settles everything," said First Minister Shen. He seemed impatient as the conversation was coming to an end. "I look forward to hearing updates from both of you."

"Marc, come by the Vertellica lobby tomorrow after lunch. From now on you'll be working half your days at Nutricorps, and the other half with us," Rishad said.

"I suppose Ashley and I will be able to handle most things in the Garden," Greg said with a hint of reluctance. He clearly didn't want to spend more time in the Garden with Ashley. "And you're always just a call away anyways, just in case we really screw something up." He gave his usual smile.

Marc didn't say anything. He didn't know what to say. He didn't have a choice in the matter. He would much rather do agritech research than sit in his apartment all day, that much he knew.

"Great! Meeting adjourned. Have a great night everybody and we'll talk soon," First Minister Aran concluded as he stood up. Marc stood up to take his leave. He made his way towards the door as First Minister Shen made one last comment.

"Oh, and Marc, make sure to behave yourself." He gave a friendly wink and smile.

Marc continued out the door and headed home.

9

arc's morning began with his usual work in the Garden. He introduced Ashley to the complexities of nutrient mixing and resource calculations so that she would be more self-sufficient while Marc was working with Vertellica. Even Greg tagged around for parts of the morning, trying to learn so that he could attempt to help Ashley in Marc's absence.

The day was halfway over when Marc made his way to Vertellica with a bag of agritech tools. He walked into the same tinted double doors that Lian had previously brought him through. There was a receptionist with a headset sitting at the front desk when he walked in. She looked up at Marc.

"Hi Marc, I'll let John know you're here and he should be up shortly." She looked down and tapped on her desk a few times.

"Thank you." Marc turned around to look around the space. There were no seats for him to wait in so he walked to the nearest wall and leaned on it. As soon as he made himself comfortable, John Riley came into the lobby.

"Marc, good to see you. Are you ready to get started?"

"I guess so," Marc answered without confidence.

"Alright, well let's get to it then. We have our work cut out for us." John turned to walk back through the doors he appeared from and beckoned for Marc to follow.

Marc pushed off against the wall and followed in John's footsteps.

"I'll take you to the lab first, so you can see what all we're working with," John said while looking back at Marc. Marc increased his pace so as to walk next to him, rather than behind him.

"The lab on the surface?" Marc asked.

"Yes and no," John answered. "See, our new lab is actually two separate labs, connected via an airlock system. So we have a full setup inside and a smaller scale lab outside. We should be able to do most of our work without going up to the surface."

"I see," Marc said. He looked around the halls as they walked. It was a labyrinth of twists and turns and vast hallways.

John looked at Marc and noticed him looking around with an unhappy demeanor.

"Listen, Marc," John began speaking with his voice lowered. "I know things are a little uncomfortable right now because of the whole 'break in' situation and I know how the First Minister can be. But you and I have the chance to do some really important work here that would be great for the colony."

"Do you actually think all this is possible?" Marc stared carefully at John to try to measure the sincerity of his answer.

"To be honest, I don't know. What I do know is that we're probably the best chance at a future for everyone in this colony." John stopped walking when they approached a metal door.

Marc saw an earnestness in John that he didn't expect. He nodded in acknowledgment of the answer.

"Here we are," John said while placing his hand on the door. It slid open. "You should be able to access the lab without me if you ever need to, I had Rishad add your biometrics."

"Thanks. I guess we won't need each other's help all the time. I don't think I can help with the genetic engineering," Marc said as they both passed into the lab.

"And I'm far from an agritech expert," John smiled amiably. "This is the lab we'll spend most of our time in."

Marc looked around. He saw lab benches with every piece of equipment imaginable. He saw liquid handlers, thermocyclers, incubators, scales, microscopes, assorted glassware, additive manufacturers, and more. Most of it looked to be automatable.

"Impressive," Marc said as he began to walk around the space, examining everything familiar and unknown. He placed his bag of agritech tools on a benchtop and laid them out. John watched him as he removed one gardening utensil after another from the bag. He reached for one and picked it up.

"Is this just a knife?" John asked, examining the sharp metal blade.

"A gardening knife," Marc clarified. "It's actually called a hori hori. Extremely versatile when starting or maintaining plants."

"I see." John set the tool down in the neat row Marc had formed. "Vertellica told me to make a list of what I needed, so I listed every piece of equipment I could think of, whether I could think of a use for it or not." John was smil-

ing as if he enjoyed taking advantage of Vertellica's resources. "I even had this table custom built." He walked up
to the table in the center of the lab and Marc approached
across from him.

The table was made of a matte metal and was a circle of
about 2 meters in diameter. It was a solid block with no legs.
The top went straight to the floor.

"Is it some kind of fancy lab bench or what?" Marc
asked.

"Not quite," John answered, still smiling. He tapped on
the circle towards the edge and a small screen appeared. A
home icon was clearly visible and he touched it. "Watch
this."

Marc stood, watching the table closely. It began to move.
Not side to side but up and down. The top surface of the
table shifted so that a landscape appeared in three dimen-
sions. There were metallic hills, mountains, valleys, ridges,
and canyons.

"Recognize what you see?" John asked. Marc stood mo-
tionless while examining the scenery. "We call it the geotable."

"Is this…" he didn't know how to finish the sentence.

"Yes," John helped him. "It's a three-dimensional repre-
sentation of the colony. Or rather, the natural features above
it, since we're underground."

"That's amazing," Marc said while taking a few steps to the side to get a view from another angle.

"Yes, it's quite the engineering feat. We've taken scans of the entire planet over the years, and this table is capable of displaying any part of it." John tapped around on the control panel and the table shifted to a new landscape almost instantaneously. A sharp narrow peak with five distinct points emerged towards the outside of the table's edges.

"Where's that?" Marc asked in awe of the landscape.

"Our planet imaging team named this the Ridge of Daggers," John responded. "It's one of my favorite features on the planet."

"I can see why." Marc reached out towards the peaks.

John quickly grabbed Marc's arm before he could make contact. "The actual ridge narrows to just inches at the points, Marc. And this is a much smaller scale."

Marc looked at John with some confusion while lowering his hand.

"I'm saying if you put your hand too close you might cut yourself. It's that sharp." John changed the landscape back to the previous location as he concluded his warning.

"Did you design it?" Marc reached out and touched a dull mountain to feel its stability.

"No," John laughed. "I just came up with the idea and I had some Vertellica engineers create the designs back on

Earth. They transmitted the plans to the Fabrication Corporation and they made it for me. It's made of millions of nanoscopic metal cylinders that push up or down based on directed magnetic impulses. The impulses, of course, depend on the input information. The cylinders can even curve based on the signals they receive."

"Fascinating," Marc said as he was done touching the table and looked back at John.

"Yes, it's quite something. I thought it could help us to plan out agricultural setups after we find a way to grow something." John tapped again near the edge of the table and it leveled out to resemble an ordinary metal table.

"I guess we should figure that out then," Marc laughed. He liked John. He seemed honest enough and like Marc, he was passionate about innovation.

"Where do you want to begin?" John asked him.

"I guess we should pick a plant to work with. But for that I need a little more information on what we're working with here."

"That's what I was thinking too. This morning, I actually went out to the surface and collected a soil sample." John was one step ahead.

"Have you analyzed it yet?"

"Yes, I did some chromatography but I haven't looked at the results yet. I wouldn't really know how to interpret them as to what we have or need." John made a movement towards some instruments on one side of the room with a quick pace.

"Great, John. Let me see what we've got." Marc followed John to a screen displaying an analysis of the soil contents. "There's no organic matter, which is a problem but one that's expected."

"Also no water," John added. "As I'm sure you know, most of the water on this planet is in the form of ice crystals underneath the surface. They melt during the day and refreeze at night."

"Right, that's going to be an issue." Marc continued to look at the screen. "There is a surprising amount of minerals, but still not nearly enough to support a plant. This is going to be tough."

"Well, I hear you're the best, Marc. So I'm optimistic." John said.

"That makes one of us." Marc didn't like the soil. An unknown number of years of no organic life means a massive lack of nutrients.

John and Marc both stood silent, contemplating their options.

"I think I know how we can get water," John said.

"Well get as much as you can, we're going to need it," Marc responded. "I'm thinking about the organic matter that we'll need. Do you think we could get the Waste Management Department to help us add nutrients to the soil?"

"I think that would be manageable," John said. "So if we get that, what else do we need?"

"Let's start with that and go from there," Marc said.

"I'll make a few calls and see what I can do," John said while making mental notes. "While I do that, do you think you would be able to pick a plant or two you would want to try to grow?"

"Sure, do you have a list of the options or should I go back to Nutricorps to find one?" Marc asked.

"Check that minus 80 over there," John pointed at a metal door with a large latch. "We should have everything you have at Nutricorps and then some." John began walking out of the lab.

Marc made his way to the door and pulled the latch open to reveal a massive walk-in freezer almost as big as Marc's apartment. He took a few steps in and realized that the entire left side was stocked with dehydrated seed packets. *This is the largest seed bank I've ever seen*, he thought to himself.

He wiped snow and ice off of labels while foraging through the seeds, hoping that one would catch his eye. He even saw the same maroon *Rafflesia aerobia* seeds he had brought with him.

Then he found one packet of small seeds. It was labeled *Pseudotsuga menzeli*. Marc examined the packet and smiled. *The Adams-Fir*, he thought. *Perfect*.

He walked out of the freezer, thankful to be back in the warmth, and placed the seed packet on one of the lab benches. He made sure to go back and relatch the freezer door.

He tapped on the bench, expecting a screen to appear. Nothing showed. He tapped another spot, then another, another.

"What are you doing, Marc?" John walked back in and angled his head with confusion.

"I was trying to use the desk screen."

"Oh, the lab benches with black tops don't have screens built in. Just the desks with gray tops."

"Oh, I see," Marc responded feeling embarrassed.

"I made a couple of calls to the Waste Management Department and Leto's Best about our problems and they both said they can help."

"Leto's Best?" Marc asked.

"Yes, they told me that with the help of the Department of Expansion, they'll be able to install a water reservoir right by the surface lab. They weren't sure how much water they would be able to provide, but they seemed confident it would be enough."

"That's great!" Marc didn't expect such a quick solution.

"And the Waste Management Department is going to begin funneling all of the nutrients they don't send to Nutricorps right here to us."

"That was easier than I thought it would be," Marc said to John. "Thanks for figuring all that out."

"That's part of what I'm here for," John responded. "Did you have any luck picking a plant?"

"Yes, I did!" Mark said excitedly. "It's not going to provide any food for the colony, but it should be a good start."

"What is it?" John asked. He picked up the packet of seeds and read aloud. "Pseudot..." he began to attempt the pronunciation.

"The scientific name is *Pseudotsuga menzeli*, but the common name is the Adams-Fir. It's technically not a true fir, but it's an extremely efficient oxygen producer, and it can survive darkness for extended periods of time, if necessary. On top of that, I know that there can be a lot of genetic variations within the species, which I thought might be of benefit to you." Marc finished his explanation.

"Sounds great, more genetic diversity means more potential for enhancement. How fast does it grow?"

"I would say probably a few feet per year, but it's hard to say here," Marc answered.

"Alright then, I think we've made some good steps towards progress today. I'll do some research into it's genetics. I'll see if there's enough background research that already exists so I can figure out ways to enhance its ability to live on the surface. Maybe even make it grow faster."

"Anything else I should do in the meantime?" Marc asked.

"I think that until we get the reservoir and some nutrients we're probably at a standstill. Feel free to head out early or go back to Nutricorps."

"Perfect, I'll head out then and let you get to your research."

"See you soon, Marc."

10

ater that evening, Marc found himself at the Game Bar taking advantage of the drink special that the mustached Advisory Council member had previously mentioned. With everything going on, he was taking time to relax. Halfway through his glass of Leto's Best Slump, he entered into the Blockade tournament and played against an older woman, as well as a little boy. Both games progressed smoothly in Marc's favor. First beating the older woman by commanding a close circling blockade to surround her Distractors and Runner. She smiled a calm nod of defeat towards Marc as she slowly got to her feet and waddled away.

The game against the little boy was trickier. The boy was aggressive in commanding his Blockers against Marc's Distractors. Marc used the aggression to his advantage and led the boy into a trap which rendered him unable to prevent Marc's Runner from escaping unchallenged. The little boy quickly went to tears after losing and ran out of the bar quickly. His disappointed parents started after him and called out his name. Soon Marc stood around the bar, studying faces until he would be set up with his next game. Then he saw a familiar figure across the room.

"Lian!" Marc called out as he jogged a few steps towards her. He reached out and touched her forearm as she was mid-stride facing the opposite direction. She spun around quickly.

"Marc!" she exclaimed with surprise. "I haven't seen you since we were taken to my father's place. Where have you been?"

"He ended up having me attend the Advisory Council meeting where he put me on a research project with Vertellica as a punishment," Marc responded.

"Oh that's too bad," Lian commented. "Are you working in that renovated lab they just finished working on?"

"That's the one," he answered. "It's the fanciest lab I've ever seen, but then again, I've spent most of my time working outdoors."

"I had to deliver a lot of the equipment there so I know exactly how fancy it is," she laughed. "I even spent some time playing around with that cool landscape desk. Have you used that?"

"That thing is unbelievable," Marc smiled. "John calls it the geotable."

"Hmm I don't know. I think landscape desk has a better ring to it," Lian joked.

"I don't know about that," Marc laughed. "What ended up happening to you at Aran's place?"

"Oh, he just scolded me like fathers do. He said if I do anything else he'll make me work in the Waste Management Department."

"Oh yikes," Marc laughed. "I couldn't picture a girl like you working in a place like that." Lian smiled.

"A girl like me?" she asked for clarification. Marc started blushing and paused before getting any more words out.

"Uh, yes," he stuttered. Flirting was never his forte. "I just mean…"

"Relax, Marc," Lian interrupted. "I'm just messing with you." She laughed as she brushed her hair behind her ear. Marc laughed uncomfortably.

"So how are you doing in the tournament?" Lian asked.

"I won my first two games. How many games are there?"

"Usually there's four. But that's with a usual turnout. I haven't checked the bracket yet but it seems like there are a lot more people here tonight." Lian looked around the room to do a quick head count.

"That might just be for the drink deal," Marc added.

"I see you're taking advantage of that," Lian said, examining the empty cup in Marc's left hand. "Maybe I should too." She took a few quick steps towards the bar as Marc followed. Soon enough she had a drink in her hand and passed a second to Marc.

"Thanks," Marc said, glad to have his hand occupied once more.

"Just be careful, Marc," Lian warned. "Remember, they may go down easy but they're strong. Like you'll be 'Slumped' with just a few drinks strong." Marc laughed at the pun.

"I think I can handle it," he replied confidently, recognizing the same warning she gave last time. Lian looked at him skeptically.

"I think I'm up," she said as she walked towards a Blockade table. Her opponent was standing next to the table with both hands behind his back. She pointed to his left side as he showed his hand to reveal the Runner in his palm.

"I'll take the Blockade," she decided. Marc made his way to the side of the table to observe. Lian gave him a wink and then looked at the black and orange board. She made her first move as her opponent took his seat.

There was a quick answer. Marc watched in awe at the game. Both players seemed to have a deep understanding of strategy. The opponent took a calculated approach, taking a short moment to consider multiple actions. Lian was the exact opposite, acting impulsively to each action. She reacted to his moves almost immediately.

Move after move, capturing piece after piece. The game was over in a matter of minutes. Lian was the victor. She didn't celebrate or gloat. She nodded and smiled to her opponent and then looked at Marc as he was finishing his drink.

"That was so fast!" he said, bringing his empty glass down.

"It was," she responded with satisfaction. "Karl always tries to think ten moves in advance. It never works." She smirked.

"Was that your second game?" Marc asked.

"Third," Lian answered. "I think the next one is the final but I'll have to check the bracket."

"Maybe I'll see you there," Marc said, his optimism higher than usual.

"Maybe," she laughed. "I'll go check the screen but it looks like you're playing over there next." She pointed to a table across the room where a few people had crowded around a seated player.

"I'll head over after I grab another drink," he waved his empty glass. "Do you want one?" Lian looked to her own glass on the Blockade table, barely touched.

"I'm good for now."

Marc turned to walk towards the bar and bumped into the game table. Lian chuckled as she turned her own way to check on the bracket.

When they met up again, Marc was sitting across from his new opponent and Lian was spectating from the side. The game began after he guessed the wrong hand and his opponent elected to be the Smuggler.

He looked at the pieces as they seemed to move by themselves. Laughing, he moved his first Blocker. His opponent responded and the two traded moves back and forth. Lian watched the game with confusion. After several actions, she bent down next to Marc.

"What are you doing? You're giving her a clear path out."

"Am I?" Marc gave a long blink and examined the board with apparent confusion.

"Just watch out," Lian said as she resumed her previous position next to the table.

Marc took another sip of Slump as his opponent saw the opening. The Runner slid to the opposite side of the board.

Marc moved one of his Blockers adjacent to it. His opponent moved the Runner to a new piece by one of Marc's other Blockers. He sat silently giggling to himself. The Slump was quickly getting to him.

He moved another Blocker to the opposite side of the Runner, blocking off the reverse movement. His opponent displayed confusion and again moved the Runner. Marc continued to laugh while he moved Blocker after Blocker after the Runner. It was a game of cat and mouse.

Lian shook her head and smiled as she saw the trap that Marc had somehow laid. He won the game quickly after.

"That was," Lian began, not knowing how to continue. "Interesting, to say the least." Marc patted her on the shoulder as he stood up with his drink.

"I had that planned the whole time," he bragged.

"Sure you did," Lian expressed her doubt as he stumbled a few steps. "I guess it's us in the final. If you make it till then." She mumbled the last sentence to herself.

"Are you scared?" Marc was slurring his words now. Lian put her arm around his shoulder. He placed his hand around her hip. She guided him towards the final table where several people were crowded. When they arrived across the room they sat down opposite each other.

"Can I have some of this?" Lian asked, grabbing Marc's drink off the table. He gave a violent nod and some heavy blinks. She took it and pretended to take a sip before placing the rest on a table behind her, away from Marc.

"Here we go, Marc," Lian said loudly, as if trying to keep him engaged. She moved one of her Blockers. The board was spinning as Marc looked down towards his pieces. He grabbed one and made a quick move.

The rest of the game was a blur.

11

Marc woke up suddenly as the bright light hit his eyes. He squinted when he sat up and rubbed his throbbing head. His eyelids did the hard work to stay open.

Where am I? Marc looked around at his surroundings. He was sitting on a couch in the same clothes he wore to the Blockade tournament. He was in a living room with two other couches and multiple wall screens. Next to the living room was a kitchen vaguely similar to his own, but with no plants growing on the counter. He noted a small black side table next to the couch he was on. There was a note on a small screen and a cup with an unknown liquid in it.

```
Marc, I tried to wake you before I
left for work but I couldn't. Drink
this theanoid and you'll feel bet-
ter.
```

There wasn't a signature so Marc's confusion continued to build. He followed the note's instructions and lifted the cup. He tilted his head back and sucked down the liquid. He cringed at the salty taste.

After setting the cup back on the side table, Marc stood up from the couch. When he rose, he took a few steps towards the nearest screen. It displayed the time.

I'm late for work! he realized with shock. *Very, very late.* He began to make his way towards the door but looked down to realize he was only wearing one sock and one shoe. And the sock was on the foot without the shoe.

"That doesn't make any sense, Marc," he said aloud to himself. "What were you doing?"

He fixed his footwear situation and continued his way towards the door. On the way out he noticed a shelf with a small framed screen scrolling through photos. Marc saw a photo of Lian's Hexball team, followed by a photo of Lian and the First Minister. *Oh this is Lian's apartment.*

Marc walked out of the sliding door and made his way to the magnet rail. He went straight to work. He walked in the main entrance to Nutricorps and saw Ashley focused on her desk screen. She looked up and started smiling.

"How are you feeling?" she asked, holding back laughter.

"What do you mean?" Marc responded, trying to act like nothing was out of the ordinary.

"Oh, I see it's worse than I thought," she was laughing now.

"What's so funny?" Marc asked, confused.

"You don't remember, do you?"

"Remember what?"

"I saw you last night," Ashley started. "And we had a conversation. Well, kind of."

"Oh no. Do I want to know how it went?" Marc could see that Ashley was enjoying this.

"I'm going to tell you even if you don't."

"Alright then," Marc said. "Let's hear it." He didn't know whether to feel scared or embarrassed or a combination of the two.

"I ran into you in the middle of the recreation center. I think it was right after you played the final game of Blockade in the tournament because that's what you were yelling about."

"Were you watching the game?" Marc asked, trying to understand the scene.

"No, I was leaving the Experience Plaza because my experience got delayed until tomorrow for some reason. I saw you on my way back to my apartment and thought I'd come over to see what you were yelling about."

"And what was that about?"

"You yelled 'I thought I had you!' and 'Did you cheat?' and stuff along those lines," Ashley said, still laughing. "I guess you lost to Lian and weren't happy about it."

"Oh, that's not as bad as I thought it would be," Marc admitted.

"Oh, I'm not finished, Marc," she continued. She was clearly enjoying his discomfort. "When I came and asked if you were alright, Lian was practically carrying you and your eyes were barely open."

"Did I say anything bad when you came over?" Marc began to worry again. It's never a good feeling to hear your life being retold to you as if you weren't there, he thought.

"Nothing too bad," Ashley confessed. "But you said something like 'Hey Ashley! Isn't Lian really pretty?' so of course I went along with it. You repeated it a few times."

"Oh, great," Marc was thoroughly embarrassed at this point. "Please tell me that's all that happened."

"Yeah that's pretty much everything," Ashley said. "Lian said she would take you back to sleep so I figured you would be fine." She was still smiling.

"I'm sorry you had to see that," Marc said while shaking his head. "The drinks here are clearly stronger than the ones I had back on Earth."

"Don't worry about it, Marc," Ashley said to try to make him feel better. "It happens to everyone."

"Does it?" Marc's eyebrows raised.

"Umm not really."

"Great," he laughed to try to force the pain away. "Thanks for catching me up, Ashley."

"I'd be happy to do it again," she laughed. Marc gave a sarcastic smile back to her and he walked through the door and back to his office space. He took a seat at his desk and started touching around on his screen. He checked the plant nutrient and water levels and checked to make sure all of the light patterns were consistent. Everything seemed to be in perfect order. *Ashley's picking this up quick*, Marc thought.

He looked at the time on the corner of his screen. His day was already almost halfway over. He had just gotten to Nutricorps, and because of his tardiness he already needed to leave for Vertellica.

Suddenly, Ashley's voice came through the desk.

"Marc, there's a really pretty girl here to see you," she said while unsuccessfully holding back more laughter.

She's never going to let me forget that.

The door to the lobby opened up and Lian came walking in. Marc noted that she looked gorgeous, as always. She walked up to Marc and hopped up to sit on his desk.

"How are you feeling?" she asked.

"I actually don't feel terrible. Physically at least, mentally it's a different story."

"Well, you're halfway there then," she said with a beautiful smile. "Ashley said she filled you in a little?"

"Yep, she told me how I acted like a fool and could barely walk."

"Do you remember the game at all?" Lian asked while adjusting to a more comfortable position.

"Honestly, not really. I remember sitting down at the table with a bunch of people around but that's where things got fuzzy." Lian laughed.

"Well maybe that's for the best," she said.

"It was that bad?"

"It wasn't great, but it wasn't anything that anyone will be upset about. People just thought it was entertaining to watch."

"I guess that's good," Marc said with the inflection of a question.

"I just wanted to come and check in on you. I told you a few times last night that the Slump will sneak up on you."

"That's for sure. I should've listened."

"Well," Lian said standing up from the desk. "I have to get going. Let me know if you need anything. I can always point you towards more salinic stimulants if you need them."

"Is that what that drink was? I thought it tasted salty." Marc moved his tongue around his mouth remembering the feel of the liquid.

"Yes," Lian laughed again. "It's great for perking you back up and flushing out whatever Slump is still in your system."

"I see."

"I'll see you around, Marc." Lian smiled at him as she walked back through the door to the lobby and left Nutri-corps.

Marc sat around in his chair for a few minutes to wallow in his pool of embarrassment. After he got his mental strength back, he left for the Vertellica lab.

He placed his hand on the lab door and it slid open. John was sitting at a biosafety cabinet, holding a pipette.

"Marc," John said without looking up from his work. "I heard you had a rough night."

Does everyone in the colony know about last night? Marc asked himself.

"So they tell me," he said while walking up next to John.

"Leto's Slump isn't exactly the Bloom Lites you're probably used to back on Earth." He ejected a tip from the pipette and set it down to look at Marc.

"You know about Bloom Lites?" Marc asked with surprise. John turned from his biosafety cabinet to face Marc.

"Yes, I would say almost every adult in Makan does. Leto's Best made a special shipment from Earth a few years back."

"I had no idea."

"I can't believe people drink that stuff. It tasted terrible." John picked up a few microcentrifuge tubes and placed them in a rack on a shaker. "It was so carbonated."

"I never minded it. Maybe it doesn't travel well."

"Maybe."

"So what are you working on?" Marc switched the conversation topic.

"I'm glad you asked, Marc," he began. "After you left yesterday, I was looking through the Vertellica data hub and I actually found a lot of interesting studies done on the Adams-Fir, and plant genetics in general. I found a gene that's present in all plants that's one of the major regulators of photosynthesis. Some studies showed that the expression of the gene directly correlates to the rate at which it releases oxygen. By using that gene as a control point, I'm inserting additional promoters as well as upregulators to the operon." John looked to Marc to see if he was understanding. Marc had a confused look on his face.

"And what exactly will that do?" Marc asked.

"Picture the gene like a lightbulb, but instead of producing light, it's making oxygen. Say that a lightbulb is turned on by a switch, or a promoter. By adding more switches, the lightbulb has a greater chance of being turned on, meaning that it will be easier for oxygen to be made." John finished his explanation.

"That makes sense," Marc responded. "So you're basically making it easier for the Adams-Fir to produce oxygen?"

"Exactly, Marc," John showed his excitement. "Not only this, but I'm inserting many additional copies of these gene units into the plant so that not only is it easier for it to produce the oxygen, it will produce more of it in general."

"That's amazing, John!" Marc didn't have a complete understanding of genetics but John helped him to understand this important alteration. It was very helpful.

"There is one downside, but I think we can overcome it," John stated.

"What's that?" Marc asked.

"We're essentially giving these plants a faster metabolism," John said.

"So we're going to need more nutrients and water per plant than expected." Marc connected the dots. Marc stopped to think for a moment while John continued to work with his gloved hands.

"I should be able to artificially encapsulate the seed prototypes and have them germinating by the end of the day," John continued. "Afterwards you can plant it and see how it performs. I haven't the faintest idea of how to judge plant health."

"You're making fast progress. Seems like we'll be able to see if the concepts translate into reality. Of course, these changes may alter growth rate so that should be interesting to study," Marc responded with optimism.

John and Marc talked about their work and educated each other about their respective fields of science. The two exchanged knowledge of genetics and agritechnology so that they could work together seamlessly. Their work progressed as John finished editing the plant stem cells and getting them to rapidly proliferate before encapsulating them to form what appeared to be a typical seed.

When their work was finishing up, two men came walking through the lab doors carrying large boxes. They were both clad in navy boilersuits. They gave a nod of acknowledgment and walked past Marc and John and to the back of the lab. They opened the door to the airlock and placed the boxes on the ground before leaving the way they entered.

John noticed Marc staring.

"They're from the Department of Expansion. They're going to build the reservoir on the surface lab."

"I guess things move quickly around here," Marc said.

"Things certainly move forward with all of Vertellica's money and power. It's a blessing and a curse." John seemed aggravated by what he said.

"What do you mean by that?" Marc asked.

"Nothing really," John responded. Then he lowered his voice. "Sometimes I just feel like Vertellica is doing important science, but at too great an expense. They don't always have the most ethical approaches."

Marc was surprised at John's negative outlook about the very company he worked for.

"Like keeping the oxygen level below what it is on Earth?" Marc asked.

"That's part of it, but I can't really talk about much more." John bent his neck to look all around the room. "If you want my advice, go to the data hub and look up Project Magellan." He looked Marc in the eyes with a serious gaze. "It's all about oxygen levels for the population so it's related to our work." John winked.

"I'll look into that," Marc said, showing his uncertainty. He recognized the project name from talking to Lian and First Minister Shen but never got any of the details.

"I got you personal access to most of Vertellica, though it took some convincing," John added. "You now have access to the same room you got in trouble for going in. Funny how things work out. The doors are double secured and you don't have your own passcode but you can use mine. It's 6-8-4-5-6."

Marc nodded and turned away from John to leave the lab. He wandered back through the Vertellica labyrinth. He took a few turns and backtracked a couple times until he eventually found the door to the room Lian had first brought him to.

He looked at the numbers displayed by the door. He typed in the code John had given him.

6-8-4-5-6.

After entering the code, a red X displayed. He tried again. No luck. He thought back to what John had said. John had to ask to get Marc access and said it was double secured. *Is it biometric*? Marc asked himself.

He placed his hand on the door. Nothing happened. He tried typing in the code again while leaving his palm against the door. Sure enough, it slid open. The door seemed to require both an access code and a biometric pass.

Interesting, Marc thought. He walked into the room and made his way to the many screens against the wall. He tapped on the desk screen when he approached and it lit up with a keyboard. He typed into it.

The wall screens turned on and the central display showed a table of percentages.

```
Surface Air Composition.
Nitrogen 81.8%, Oxygen 13.7%, Carbon
dioxide  0.8%,  Argon  1.3%,  Trace
2.4%.
```

Marc made a mental note of the values before continuing his research. The oxygen was low and the carbon dioxide was high. Very high.

He then searched for Project Magellan. The computer prompted him to enter an access code. He typed in the numbers John gave him. Under the main link there were several others. He tapped on the related links to reveal experimental data. He read through article after article about the effects of an altered oxygen supply.

He did more research and clicked on related links one after the other. Finally, he was brought to another study referencing much smaller sample sizes. Marc tapped around to control the screens and expand the data for better visualization. What he saw surprised him.

```
Effect of rapidly decreased Oxygen
and increased Carbon Dioxide on hu-
man survivability.
Environmental  Adjustment  Periods
Tested:  3  months,  6  months,  12
months,  18  months,  24  months,  36
months.
Patients Tested Per Condition: 3.
Patient Ages: REDACTED.
Testing Facility: REDACTED.
Results: REDACTED.
```

Most of the information from the experiment was re-dacted but the takeaway was clear to Marc. Vertellica was conducting human experiments to see how fast they could force people to evolve to live on the surface.

He closed out of the system and left Vertellica in a hurry. He had many questions in his head and wanted unbiased answers. He needed the perspective of someone outside of Vertellica and WOSE.

12

Marc made his way to the Experience Plaza. He was on a mission to find Ashley. Her local opinion was a valuable asset to bounce thoughts off of. He entered the Experience Plaza through the classic theater style entrance with digital letters and blinking lights imitating the ones he saw as a child back on Earth.

He passed through double doors and followed along the red carpet with velvet rope guides. He smelled popcorn and saw monstrous reusable cups presumably filled with Leto's Best Cola.

Marc approached the concession stand to find a somewhat familiar, half shaven face. His name tag read *Jake*.

"Hi, I'm looking for Ashley Grisham," Marc started.

"I recognize you," Jake responded. "From the Advisory Council meeting."

"Yes, Vertellica has me working on a research project for them now." he said to try to ignore the initial reason for his attendance. "Anyways, have you seen Ashley?" Jake looked at him skeptically.

"Yeah, she's here." He looked down at a screen in front of him while scratching his half beard. "Theater six. I think she's seeing the same experience for the third or fourth time." He smiled and pointed around the side of the concessions.

"Thanks," Marc said and followed the continuing carpet with popcorn crumbs scattered throughout. He walked down the dimly lit hallway with experience advertisements in digital frames along each wall. He approached a lit up 6 and wandered through the heavy pull door and into the darkness of the room. He could barely see his feet below him as he walked in.

Suddenly he came across a flash of light that made him appear to be seated in some kind of vehicle. He looked around him and saw that he was high off the ground in what looked like a park back on Earth. He stumbled backwards as the ground started to move much closer. It was as if he was in a crashing shuttle.

"Hey careful, the motion simulators are about to kick in," a familiar voice rang out and cut through the scene.

"Ashley?" Marc called out while turning his neck in all directions.

"Marc?" came the response. He felt a hand grab his wrist from behind as Ashley managed to guide him into a seat next to her. "You seem lost."

"Actually, I was looking for you." He grabbed the seatbelt and fastened it over himself as he bobbed around helplessly in the moving chair.

"Oh really? You came to the right place." The inflection in her voice changed, indicating she was smiling while talking.

"Can I ask you some questions about growing up here?" Marc asked with a friendly yet businesslike attitude.

"Of course, Marc. Let me just pause this." The scene around them faded away and the room lit up with a warm orange light. The room was smaller than Marc thought. There were six chairs attached to mechanical arms that came from the ground. Marc and Ashley sat in the middle two seats while the rest were vacant.

"So what do you want to ask about?" Ashley kept the conversation going while Marc continued to study the room around him. He turned towards her to meet her curious eyes.

"Remember when I asked you about growing up here, and you talked about applying for jobs and how you would never apply to Vertellica?"

"Yeah," she said looking to the side to recount the interaction. "I remember. What about it?"

"Why is that?" He wanted to avoid diving too far too fast.

"It's like my dad always said," she began. "Never trust anyone who locks all their doors to the public."

"I've never heard you mention your dad," Marc commented.

"He died eight years ago," Ashley responded with sad eyes.

"I'm sorry to hear that."

"Thanks, Marc. He was a really passionate man, and I think a lot of that got passed down to me. He hated Vertellica."

"Why did he hate Vertellica?"

"When I was growing up he actually was a scientist working for them. They were doing all kinds of experiments on acquired diseases that people get even after being genetically modified against them."

"Epigenetics?" Marc asked.

"Yes, I think that's right," she continued. "I haven't heard the term for a while but he had to work with a bunch of animals and give them diseases just so they could study their biology. He really hated it."

"So he quit to get away from killing animals?"

"It wasn't quite that. He told me that they wanted him to do some crazy experiments that he didn't agree with. I heard the term parabiosis a lot but I never really understood what it was." Ashley looked at Marc inquisitively.

"Parabiosis is combining living things together. In plants, we call them grafts. But if he was working with animals..." Marc trailed off for a minute. "They would probably be surgically connecting them together to share a circulatory system, similar to xylem and phloem in plants." Ashley looked at him with concern.

"Oh," she said. "So that's why he quit."

"It's not a very ethical way of conducting animal research," Marc admitted. "Especially in this day and age."

"And after he left they made it difficult for him to find decent work. The colony being as small as it is and Vertellica having so much pull." Ashley looked away for a moment. "My dad used to say, 'Corporations are as powerful as nations but are better at hiding their secrets.'" Ashley made her voice deeper to portray her father's voice.

"Did your mother feel the same way?" Marc asked while giving a brief smile at her imitation.

"No idea," she responded. "She died when I was born. So much progress has been made in healthcare yet I lost both parents too young. Makes you think." She looked towards the ground as if getting lost in her own thoughts.

"I know how you feel," Marc placed his hand on her shoulder to comfort her. She looked at his face and immediately knew that he meant it.

"So anyways," she tried to brighten her own mood. "Is that all you wanted to ask about?"

"Well, the truth is," he started slowly, unsure of how to continue. He glanced around to make sure they were alone. "I think Vertellica is hiding some things. And I wanted to see if I could talk to you about it."

"Of course, Marc. What kind of things do you think they're hiding," Ashley asked, her curiosity piqued. Marc hesitated again, looking around the empty room once more.

"What is it?" She noticed his discomfort.

"Human experiments," he finally added.

"Human experiments?"

"Yes, I found some data they partially covered up."

"What did it say?" Ashley asked.

"Not much, honestly. It was mostly redacted. But it hinted at human experiments being run in order to rapidly force people to live in the atmospheric conditions on the surface."

"Did you see any of the experiments?" Ashley was confused.

"No, but I'm going to try to find them. Or at least find out some more information."

"Do you want help?" she was quick to offer.

"No," Marc began. "I think I have someone else on my side that wants to find out just as bad as I do." He showed quiet confidence.

"Then it seems like you have things figured out for now," Ashley responded. She remained serious. "You'll have to let me know what you find out. I know my dad would want me to do anything I can to help you."

"Of course, Ashley," Marc smiled at her sincerity. "You'll be the first to know."

"Can I ask you a personal question, Marc? It's not really related," she seemed perplexed by something.

"Of course."

"Why aren't you genetically enhanced?"

Marc was caught off guard by the question. He needed a moment to gather his thoughts and switch focus.

"I grew up in a wealthy area back on Earth. The problem was that my parents had no money. They worked as landscapers for the rich houses and apartments in my district, but they were never paid well. They couldn't afford to have me enhanced, just like they couldn't afford to give me any siblings after I was born. I started working with them, gardening when I was just a little kid. So I could help out and bring in some money. I went to school with the kids whose yards I worked in and they never let me forget it." Marc was looking away from Ashley as he remembered his rough childhood.

"I thought that enhancements were completely widespread and affordable back on Earth," Ashley said.

"Not when my parents were trying to have a child. Back then it was still considered a luxury to be able to enhance your child. Only the upper classes could afford it but as science advanced and laws changed, enhancements became more of a necessity."

"It sounds like a tough environment to be part of," Ashley responded sympathetically. "So you were one of the only unenhanced people around?"

"Unfortunately. I was short, I was overweight, I probably needed glasses. I was less athletic and not as smart as my classmates. There was really only one thing I was good at, and that was growing plants. Everyone around me was perfect, and I was far from it."

"But you're here now, Marc. Billions of miles away from all those people," Ashley commented, trying to get Marc to focus on the present.

"I guess you're right."

"And you're one of the smartest people I've ever met and you're definitely not short." She smiled at him and tried to boost his confidence.

"Oh, just overweight, then?" Marc forced out a small smile.

"No, no!" Ashley exclaimed. "I was…"

"I'm kidding, Ashley," he chuckled while moving on from the subject. Ashley seemed to move on too as she smiled sarcastically at his joke.

"I hope Vertellica doesn't try to make Makan like Earth." Ashley's mood shifted back to the annoyance she had when talking about Vertellica. "It seems like they're already trying to use people for their unethical agendas."

"Maybe there's a way to change things around here," Marc looked into her eyes as they lit up. "First, we need to find out what exactly they're trying to do."

13

The next morning Marc woke up and had his usual cereal with milk for breakfast. While eating, he watched the wall screen in the living room on mute. Mountain goats climbed higher and higher on virtually invisible ledges until they escaped from their predators. One kid was following the nanny to the top when Marc decided to change the channel.

There was then a news clip that he didn't expect. Rishad was seen walking through the very lab that Marc and John had been working in. His lips were moving as he moved towards the screen. Marc unmuted the screen to hear what was going on.

"...and our best scientists from Vertellica and Nutricorps are working tirelessly so that one day, we might be able to expand the colony above ground," The camera cut away from Rishad and showed a three-dimensional rendering of a green park on the planet's surface in between tan mountains. The park was surrounded with smaller buildings with porches and a large fountain sporting the Vertellica logo sat in the center. It was strangely nostalgic to the life Marc remembered back on Earth, but he knew it would seem like an alien concept to the people of the colony.

The camera cut back to the lab and zoomed in on Rishad. "I'll be providing brief updates like these periodically so make sure to tune back in. Vertellica, innovating a better life." He signed off with their famous slogan.

Marc finished his cereal while deep in thought. He makes it seem like our work will be done in a couple of years. I guess they want to keep convincing the people that they're doing good work.

The rest of the morning was business as usual. Marc and Ashley spent time in the Garden and managed to talk to Greg for a couple of minutes before he ran off to meetings with the Waste Management Department. Lian stopped by to make a delivery and Marc was able to talk her into some evening plans to practice his Blockade strategy.

Later in the day, Marc was with John in the Vertellica lab working on their project. They made significant progress in a short amount of time. All of the materials and facilities for the surface lab had been completed the previous night. The Department of Expansion, the Waste Management Department, and Leto's Best had been working nonstop to prepare the surface lab. Today Marc and John could move on to transferring their small, germinated seeds to the outside soil.

"Alright, Marc," John began as he pulled a small container out of a cooling block. "I think this is where you take over." He passed the container off to Marc with a smile of satisfaction.

"This is it?" Marc asked.

"Fresh and germinated," John responded. "Let's suit up and get those in the ground."

"Sounds good to me," Marc had a grin on his face as he grabbed a few of his agritech tools and followed John towards the airlock. They made their way towards orange lockers with black suits hanging on hooks. A matching black helmet with a gold translucent visor sat on a shelf at the top of each locker.

John took down his suit and pulled his legs on and covered his shoes, followed by his arms and latching gloves. He then pulled a zipper from the left hip and up to the metallic neck ring at the top of the suit. Marc followed along and imitated John as best he could. Next, a black flap of thin material was pulled from around the left side, covering the initial zipper and leading to its own zipper on the right side. Again, John zipped up to the neck ring and clipped the incomplete ring to itself across the front of his neck.

Finally, John removed the helmet from the locker and placed it over his head with the visor facing backwards. Once he brought it down far enough, the base caught on the neck ring at which point John rotated counterclockwise until it clicked into place with the visor in front.

Unfortunately for Marc, he had been following along too closely and put the helmet on backwards without knowing the next step.

"Hey John?" his muffled voice barely audible through the suit. He started to call again but then felt John's hands on his helmet. His head felt like it was spinning as the visor came into view and through it was John's face trying to disguise a smile. The click of the connection was felt as a vibration through the suit. Marc immediately felt air pressurize the suit tightly around him.

"Everything feel alright?" Marc heard John's voice clearly from within his helmet. "You don't want a leak in your suit. Even an improper seal could put you unconscious within minutes once you're outside."

"I think so," Marc responded while his suit was being inspected. John looked at him and brought up his wrist. There was a control screen with icons on it.

"Tap the microphone so I can hear you," John's voice came through again. Marc looked down at his own wrist to see the screen. He tapped the icon.

"Can you hear me now?"

"Yes, now I can," John answered. "Looks like you're all set, let's head into the airlock." He took a few silent steps towards the narrow door to the side of the lockers. There was a lever to the side that he pulled down with his gloved hands. The door moved away and then to the side without a sound. John moved through it.

Marc began to walk behind him with the seeds and realized how light his suit really was. Other than the added weight of the thin compressed oxygen layer surrounding the permeable inner membrane of his suit, he felt no different than when he was just wearing his own clothes. The only change was the gold tint of the visor.

Once the two were in the cylindrical airlock, John pulled a matching lever for the same door and it closed behind them. He then touched a few buttons on a screen next to the door to the surface and a light above it blinked red.

After a few moments of waiting in silence, the light began to blink green.

"Are you ready?" John looked at Marc.

"As ready as I'm going to be," he responded, feeling the tiny bumps on his forearms pop up.

John pulled the lever of the outer airlock door and it slid open to reveal a starlit valley with mountains rising on either side. The ground in front of them was notably darker than the surrounding environment.

"I see the reservoir is doing its job so far," Marc commented.

"Yes, it appears to be diffusing into the local soil well," John added.

John closed the airlock door behind them as Marc turned to look at the small silo with the Fabrication Corporation logo on the side. He made his way towards it to examine the contents. He unhinged the small metal port in the front and soil began to poor out. Mark caught some in his hand and then closed the opening. Out of habit he held the brown handful up to his face to smell its quality. He quickly realized that he couldn't smell anything through his helmet.

"How does it look, Marc?" John approached his side.

"It looks about right. Supposedly they filled the silo with the same stuff they send over to Nutricorps, mixed in with some of the surface soil. As long as it has facultative anaerobes and some nitrogen fixing mutualists it should be perfect as a start. Of course, I'll have to adjust nutrient levels over time to figure out the optimal growth conditions"

"You're the expert," John went to a small toolbox and grabbed a pail. He passed it to Marc who filled it up from the silo opening. Marc led John to a spot of soil that he visually determined to have the most appropriate moisture content.

Without words, Marc began his work. John watched carefully as he used the sharp hori hori to loosen up the planet's surface. He then set the tool aside and took a handful of soil from the pail, and mixed it in and out of the surface, spreading it evenly in a line of a few meters. Marc then used the concave blade of the hori hori to dig a drill into the soil mixture and measured out seed placements using his hand as a well-versed ruler. After setting the spaced-out seeds in the drill, he brushed loose soil back over top and lightly packed it down. He was finished in a matter of minutes.

"All set," Marc stabbed the hori hori into the ground beside him and stood up from his kneeling position.

"Already?" John's helmet gave a slight tilt of surprise.

"Yes, that's all there is to it for now," Marc laughed and brushed the remaining soil off of his hands. "Now we wait. The hard part comes with keeping it alive after it starts to grow."

Marc picked up the pail and returned it to the toolbox by the airlock. "After you," John reopened the outer door and beckoned for Marc to pass through.

"Thanks," Marc responded and entered the small cylindrical room.

John closed the door and followed his previous airlock actions in reverse, allowing the room to rebalance with the colony's atmosphere before opening the inner door. The two passed through and removed their suits, Marc taking significantly longer than John.

Marc barred his teeth with regret.

"Everything alright?" John asked after noticing Marc's distressed face.

"I left my hori hori out there," he said. He had an internal debate about suiting back up to go get it.

"Do you need it?" John asked. "If not, it'll stay right where you left it until we go back out."

"It should be fine, I guess," Marc answered.

"Did you find anything in the data hub yesterday?" John asked Marc after they were settled. "I didn't see you after you went to check it."

"I found the atmospheric composition of the surface as compared to the inside of the colony," Marc began. "As well as some information about how human physiology has been altered." Marc then hesitated.

"Something else?" John noticed Marc's expression change.

"And some redacted experiments that I didn't quite understand."

"So, you found them," John said cryptically. "I hoped you would."

"What exactly were they doing?" Marc asked.

"I don't know everything, only rumors. But what I've heard scares me."

"It seemed like human experiments were being done, or maybe started and not finished," Marc looked to John for indication of additional knowledge.

"Testing how fast they can lower oxygen without people dying," John added with a solemn look.

"Have you seen these experiments being carried out?" Marc continued to search the extent of John's information, noticing a hesitation to say too much. John remained silent for a moment.

"I haven't personally seen it, but after you left yesterday I did some digging," he was speaking low and slow. "And I think I might've uncovered where the experiments were being conducted."

"Do you think they're still being worked on?" Marc asked.

"I'm not sure, but I intend to find out. Human experiments to that extent go against everything I've known as a scientist, and I need to find out if it's true," John seemed set on his decision. He was a moral scientist, bound by the principles of traditional bioethics.

"What do we need to do?"

"I'm going to find the labs, Marc." John said decisively. Marc reacted immediately.

"I'm coming with you John, you might need my help."

"Marc, I work for Vertellica. I have access to all the facilities. Me walking around alone won't cause any suspicion." Marc recognized the point but maintained his stance.

"We can just say we're looking for something for our research. Everyone should know about the project and since we're the experts, they can't doubt when we need something." John remained wordless, taking a minute to think on what Marc had said. After a few moments of contemplation, he finally responded.

"Stem cells."

"What?" Now Marc was confused.

"We say we need stem cells, human stem cells if they need more specificity. Those are likely maintained in cultures nearby the human experiments," John nodded, acknowledging that the plan had potential. Marc was catching on to John's point with ardor.

"So if they ask why, what do we say?" he made sure to say *we* so that John had little choice but to include him. John thought to himself for another moment as Marc waited to hear his idea.

"We're going to try to fuse human stem cells with those of plants in order to enhance their metabolism by increasing the variety of nutrient forms that can be taken up," John answered.

"This should work," Marc said, optimistically. "Lead the way."

The two left their lab and followed a series of turns and passed through door after door. Marc walked at John's side as they made a final turn towards a black metallic door with a keypad.

"If my memory is correct, this should be it," John said, indicating the door.

Marc nodded and John began to type in his access code.

6-8-4-5-6.

The keypad flashed red. John tried the code again with the same result.

"I don't understand, this code gets me into every room in Vertellica," he looked at Marc and seemed worried. "Is it possible that this lab is restricted, even to me?"

"Let me try something," Marc said and began to enter a code with a hand placed on the door.

5-1-4-1-3.

The keypad flashed green and the black door slid open to the side.

"What was that?" John asked.

"First Minister Shen's access code, it must be universal and open even restricted doors," Marc began to walk in the door as John gave a look of surprise and gratitude.

"You would think if something is this restricted, you would need his biometrics too," John said. Marc shrugged.

They entered an elevator which only had one button. They pressed it and waited as they felt themselves begin to move downward. After a few moments, the elevator doors opened to a new room.

They passed into the room and saw a large control panel across the back side, as well as three glass enclosures. The sides of the room had two unmarked doors each. Marc and John made their way towards the control panel. Upon walking closer, they saw that the three glass enclosures had their light shut off.

John fiddled around at the control panel and messed with the screens until he finally pulled up some information. A header read Project Magellan.

"I think I found something," he then began to read. "Chamber one most recent experiment: limiting oxygen from 19 percent to 14 percent in a 12-month duration. Subject: 6 years, unenhanced, female." John slowed his reading. "6," he repeated while shaking his head.

"We have proof," Marc said with mixed feelings. On one hand they found what they were looking for, on the other, Vertellica was doing human experiments on children.

"Results: Unsuccessful, subject death," John finished reading and closed his eyes in despair.

Marc somberly walked up next to John, also feeling the heavy hit of the recent information. *They let the experiments get that far*, he thought. He was more sad for the fate of the child than angry at Vertellica. Still, he pushed on to read more.

"Chamber two most recent experiment: limiting oxygen from 19 percent to 14 percent in an 18-month duration. Subject: 4 years, unenhanced, male. Results: unsuccessful, subject rendered comatose." Marc shook his head and John remained deep in thought with his eyes closed. Marc felt his emotions continuing to rise to the surface on his own face.

"Chamber three experiment," Marc read on, voice wavering. "Limiting oxygen from 19 percent to 14 percent in a 24-month duration. Subject: 3 years, unenhanced, male. Results," he paused in shock. "In progress."

John's head raised up and he quickly looked about the control panel. He slammed his finger down on one of the controls and all three chambers lit up from the inside. The first two were empty. The third was not.

Marc and John looked on in awe. There, in the third chamber, was a small child. Its hair was short and scraggly as it lay curled up like an animal on a small, padded mat. The rest of the chamber contained a water spigot on the wall, a few colorful plastic shapes sitting about on the ground, and a corner with a sand pit. There was a metal slit in a door at the back.

"This can't be real," John said with stupor. The child flinched awake and looked through the glass.

"This is worse than I could've imagined," Marc added. The two stood without words as they looked at the scene, taking in the horrors of human experimentation. A child's life spent without interaction from within a small room made up of mostly cold metal and glass. The child moved an arm over its eyes as it remained on the mat.

John tapped around on the control panel trying to find any additional information which might help the current situation.

"Can we open up the chamber and get the kid out?" Marc asked. He began to look around the control panel with John. The two searched for any way to end the experiment. Marc's fingers passed over button after button until finally he came to one labeled *Open Chamber Door*.

"Found it," he said to John as he pressed it.

"Good," was the simple response. The two waited impatiently as the lights in the room changed to orange flashes and vents in the walls opened up allowing new airflow to the room. Several slow moments passed as they studied the room.

Suddenly, the child started coughing as it sat up. The coughs grew more and more violent as the small body began to convulse.

"Close it, quick!" John shouted. The child was laying on his back now and barely moved. Marc slammed the button but it was too late. There was a sharp beeping sound as the control panel displayed large digital letters that read *Atmosphere Equilibrated*.

John sprinted through the doors at the side of the room and made for the entrance to the experiment chamber. Marc followed closely behind. The door was sliding open as they reached the entrance. John was the first in as he stumbled to the ground and kneeled next to the unmoving child, testing his vitals. The child's chest didn't rise and fall, and there was no more coughing.

"How is he?" Marc asked, scared for the answer. Tears began to drip down John's face.

"He's gone." He showed disgust at his own words. Marc reluctantly accepted the words. They were quiet for a moment.

"We found what we came for," Marc said as he put his hand on John's shoulder. "We should leave."

John slowly nodded and rose to his feet. The two made their way back to their own lab in complete silence.

14

arc and John sat near the geotable, contemplating their findings. Both were in shock. Neither one had expected to find a human experiment in progress. Especially not one involving a child. And the child died.

John was sitting slouched over a lab bench with his bald head buried in his hands. Marc sat atop of a faux-wood desk with his elbows on his knees. Silence hung in the air.

Suddenly Marc corrected his posture. His thoughts had come to an end. John sensed the movement and tilted his head and looked at Marc through his fingers.

"We need to talk to Rishad," Marc said decisively. "He's the head of Vertellica for the Makan Colony, right?"

"He is but…" John began but Marc interrupted.

"So if anyone can stop the experiments, it's him. We just have to convince him." Marc made his way to his feet. John hesitated.

"Rishad has never been one to beat around the bush," John admitted as he sat up. "But what can we do if he tells us they can't stop. I never expected anything like this from him in the first place."

"We're both scientists, John." Marc was pacing around the lab in thought. "Like always, we'll collect the necessary information. Once we have that, we can find a way to convince him." He stopped his walk and looked at John. "Can you call Greg and tell him to come here?"

John nodded, shock still limiting his speech.

"And tell him to bring Ashley," Marc added. "She might be able to help us too."

While John went to work contacting Greg, Marc reached out to Lian. She was intelligent and had reason enough to care about this, so talking with her would be advantageous.

After their calls, Marc looked up to see John. John met his glance.

"Greg said they're on their way," he looked worried. He used his sleeve to wipe a bead of sweat running down his shiny head.

Soon after, Greg, Ashley, and Lian had all arrived at the lab. They all pulled seats up and Marc filled them in. He told them the effects of limiting the oxygen supply, the goal to terraform the planet, and the grotesque human experiments. John studied the three as if judging their trustworthiness as allies. He had felt all alone in his disapproval of Vertellica but now realized that there were others that shared his thoughts.

Greg listened intently, never trying to crack one of his usual jokes. Ashley's face was a kaleidoscope of evolving emotions from anger to confusion and back again. Lian attended with intelligent eyes, face rarely changing and offering the occasional question in order to get the most complete understanding.

Everyone was on the same page within minutes.

"And you're sure about all this, Marc?" Lian asked with finality.

"Absolutely," he responded. John nodded in quiet agreement.

"I can't believe they would do all that," Ashley's face was contorted showing a mixture of emotions. She showed no doubt in Marc's information.

"Right under our noses," Greg was shaking his head. "I work with these guys almost every day. Just like you, John. And I've never heard anything about this." He was suspended in disbelief as he looked John in the eyes for some sign of an elaborate prank. He found nothing.

"They tried to hide it from me, too," John responded with a tone of betrayal. "But we finally found it after who knows how long."

"It must've been months," Ashley added.

"Years," Lian corrected. "Marc and John said the studies lasted for up to 36 months."

"How could they have kept it hidden for all that time?" Greg asked.

"It was on a sublevel underneath Vertellica," Marc added. "We have as many questions as you do," Marc looked each of the three in the eyes. "And we intend to find out today. I hope all of you stick around when Rishad comes."

"There's strength in numbers," John added.

"I'm not leaving," Lian was the first to answer. She gave Marc a smile of reassurance.

"I can go find First Minister Shen. He should be involved in this one way or another," Greg added.

John nodded and Greg walked towards the door. Marc looked to Ashley who was as white as a ghost. A new thought had come to her mind.

"Whose children are they using for the experiments?" she asked, almost in tears. The others hadn't thought to ask that question. Marc moved and sat beside her and put his arm around her reassuringly.

"We don't know that yet. But we're going to do everything we can to find out," he spoke in his best calming voice. "Are you with us, Ashley?"

She looked at Marc and nodded while wiping her eyes.

"Then we're all in agreement. John, send a message to Rishad. Get him here however you need to."

And the four of them that remained waited for Rishad's arrival, contemplating all of their questions and searching for internal answers.

Sooner than expected, the lab door slid open and Rishad made his way in at a brisk pace. He slowed down when he saw everyone sitting in the lab with serious faces. He looked at John.

"Judging by the guests in the room and the fact that I'm the only one that responded, I'm going to guess that the airlock hasn't just breached," Rishad said as he caught his breath with a calm demeanor. Marc furrowed his brow and jerked his head towards John.

"You told me to get him here fast," John shrugged without regret. Marc returned his attention to the subject at hand.

"What's this about, Marc?" Rishad asked, noticing the others looking to him for direction. He reached down and adjusted his jacket sleeves in an attempt to appear in his usual professional manner.

"Project Magellan. We found human experiments going on in a Vertellica lab," Marc began, staring intensely at Rishad. Rishad looked around the room as if memorizing the faces of each person present.

"And you want an explanation," he said reluctantly. His face was troubled, but showed no sign of surprise. "The First Minister didn't expect you to stir up this much trouble, Marc. Have you talked to him about it?"

"You're in charge of Vertellica, right?" Ashley jumped in. "We wanted to hear it straight from the source." She was standing to Marc's left side.

"As some of you may know, First Minister Shen and I haven't always seen eye to eye," he looked first at John, then Lian. Marc remembered the many conversations in which First Minister Shen mentioned how much of a pain Rishad had been. "One of our biggest disagreements has always been how to go about making this barren planet into a suitable home."

"Jump ahead to the human experiments," Marc urged. Rishad put his hands up defensively but followed Marc's suggestion.

"Clearly you've seen the data or the actual experiments for Project Magellan. It hardly matters because both point to the same thing. The idea is a simple one; test how fast humans can adapt to the surface atmosphere. That way we could eventually move out from under the ground and have a 'more natural' environment." Rishad looked around the room to see if everyone was following.

"Why use humans?" John found his voice. "Why not other model organisms? You can't subject human patients to such harsh tests with little to no background research."

"Other animals were used initially. First mice, then dogs, even a cow. All shipped specially from Earth for this purpose. We even tried axolotls because of their environmental adaptability," Rishad explained, attention focused solely on John. "But you know just as well as I do, John, model organisms can only get you so far. They rarely accurately predict large scale physiological changes in humans." John's silence indicated to the others that Rishad's reasoning had merit.

"But why children?" Marc asked. Rishad was standing within the group now, together forming a small circle. Rishad winced at the question and closed his eyes for a brief moment, as if holding something back.

"It was decided that children should be the test subjects because their gene expression is more…" he paused to think of the right word. "Ductile. Compared to adults that is. They have a greater possibility of adapting to adverse conditions than those that have lived longer." Lian shook her head in silent anger.

"So you just take babies from the med bay whenever it suits your purpose?" Ashley asked with her arms crossed. "Or do you let them spend their first few years with their parents before taking them away?" Ashley's eyebrows raised with concern as she awaited the response. Rishad's face again showed pain.

"The children never know their parents. They're leftovers." John's face lit up with disgust and anger. The others looked at each other with confusion.

"No, I don't believe it," John said. "There's no way anyone would do that kind of thing."

"Sadly, it is true, John," Rishad added in a low voice. "Artificially gestated after fertilization." Lian was the first of the others to put the dots together.

"You mean they're in vitros… left over after the procedures work with other fertilized eggs?"

"Yes," Rishad's mouth opened but John's answered. "It's completely immoral."

"That's awful!" Ashley exclaimed, barely managing to fight back more tears.

Suddenly Lian's silent anger exploded as she stepped forward and shoved Rishad backwards.

He stumbled but managed to stay on his feet.

"Calm down, Lian," Rishad held his hands up in front of him.

"You're a monster," Lian shouted. The others exchanged quick glances, unsure of what to do. She maintained an aggressive pace toward Rishad.

"Lian…" Marc put his hand up as if to say stop. She didn't hear him.

Again, Lian shoved Rishad with all her enhanced strength.

His back slammed into the hibernating geotable. He recoiled with pain and grabbed his lower vertebrae. Lian didn't let up.

She held him violently against the edge of the table with her hands on his shoulders.

"Why would you do this?!" she shouted with rage as the others quickly made their way over to the table. Ashley maintained a safer distance from the action.

"Now Lian, be careful what you're doing there. We just wanted to talk to him." John tried to offer counsel.

"I didn't expect this from you, Lian," Rishad said and gave a laugh which turned into a pained cough. "I understand their naivety. But you?"

"None of us support this kind of research, Rishad," John joined in.

"But you don't understand," Rishad continued, Lian pushed him further over the table using only one hand. "I want what's best for everyone in Makan, no one above the rest. I feel the same way you do, Marc."

"Your actions say otherwise. Your research is killing both the young and the old," Lian said through clenched teeth. Rishad redirected his attention away from her.

"Listen to me, Marc. You don't know the full picture." He finished his sentence looking into Lian's eyes. A sudden fear emerged on his face. Marc cocked his head with confused anger.

"No one trusts what you have to say anymore," Lian said.

"If the First Minister wanted to stop the experiments, he…" Rishad was cut off as Lian gave him a final shove, all of her enhanced strength beating him into the table. Rishad could only catch himself on the geotable's control panel. He used it as leverage to lift himself up to continue his thought. "He would…" his hand caught on the controls.

Metal sliced the air as Rishad went silent.

The Ridge of Daggers pierced his chest, and he gave his last breath.

15

"No!" Ashley screamed hysterically. Her hands were pulling at the hair on top of her head.

Lian was frozen, eyes wide with fear.

John looked from Rishad's unmoving body and met Marc's eyes in horror.

Before anyone could process what had just occurred, the lab door slid open. Several people clad in green uniforms moved quickly with stunners in hand. Shots rang out through the room as bodies fell.

Marc hit the floor with his eyes facing the door. First Minister Shen walked in behind the security team, his disapproving eyes on Marc. Greg followed quickly behind. Marc's vision faded into darkness.

When Marc awoke, he was alone. He was lying on a hard mattress against the wall of a dark room. He was surrounded by four slick black walls with no visible door. A toilet and sink took up space in one corner. The ceiling was high with dim lights shining through metal slits.

Where am I? He sat up and rubbed his head. He had pain where his temple made contact with the lab floor.

"Hello?" he called out to no response. He gazed around the room, looking for any clues as to where he was. He found nothing in the darkness.

He began to think about the earlier events. Rishad being open about everything that was going on. He showed no signs of defending the experiments. *Could he really think that their work was the only way to benefit the people of the colony? Or did he know what they were doing was wrong?*

What had Rishad's last words been? 'If the First Minister wanted to stop the experiments he would?'

Thoughts continued to bounce through Marc's head as he replayed his memories. He ran through over and over again, mentally moving forward and backward through time. He flinched each time he pictured Rishad's death. It was too real and intense an image to even be recalled without stirring heavy feelings.

Marc came to the conclusion that they had been arrested for Rishad's murder. WOSE showed up with First Minister Shen right behind to clean up the situation. Greg brought him there.

He replayed Lian's sudden outburst of aggression. She had been relatively quiet up until that point. But that's how she operates. Even when playing Blockade, she takes in all the information before making any action, and when she does, it's game over for her opponent. Marc knew her anger built off of the fact that the entire colony oxygen level was decreased, not really the human experiments. It was the colony oxygen level that would kill her father.

Marc stood up to pace in his tiny cell. His mind kept taking him back to Lian, shoving Rishad against the geotable. Rishad seemed to be more confused about it than anything. Marc tried to remember what he said.

'I didn't expect this from you,' he recalled the line Rishad had said to Lian. You. Marc thought about how he had said it. There has to be something behind that interaction that I'm missing.

He continued to pace and think. Recalling every minute detail he could. He moved and contemplated for hours and hours making little progress.

His thoughts were suddenly interrupted.

One of the black walls brightened to reveal light and an adjacent room connected by the transforming glass. First Minister Shen was looking in at Marc.

"It's exhausting just watching you pace, Marc," he said monotonously. "Pretty soon you'll wear a line through the metal." He gave a friendly smile.

"So, Greg found you," Marc began. "Did he tell you everything?"

"Yes, he told me about the human experiments that you found. And he told me that you were going to confront Rishad about them and wanted me there."

"And Rishad told us all about it, Aran. He answered every question we asked." Marc was looking at the First Minister, trying to gauge his thoughts.

"Everything?" First Minister Shen asked.

Marc nodded.

"Interesting." The First Minister seemed deep in thought.

"So, what happens now?" Marc asked.

"You killed a man, Marc," the First Minister responded without changing expression. Marc let the words sink in. It wasn't his intention, but he certainly bore some of the guilt.

But then again, Rishad was conducting experiments on children. "You're going to spend a long, long time in this cell. As are your friends John and Ashley. Greg will take over for you at Nutricorps, with the occasional consultation of course. Your terraforming project is over."

Marc understood the situation.

"And Lian?" Marc was worried about her but knew her father wouldn't let anything happen to her.

"Don't worry, Marc," he said. "She's being held in her residence until we finish our investigation. She told us what you and the others did."

"What *we* did?" Marc's worry quickly became confusion.

"Like I said. You killed a man. She said she tried to stop you but she was outnumbered three to one. Of course we're still looking into the facts; unfortunately, the lab cameras went down during all the chaos." he eyed Marc suspiciously.

Marc was dumbfounded. Would she lie just to save her own skin? he wondered. Or is he making this up?

"I also found out that you somehow managed to use my security code to break into Vertellica labs that you weren't authorized to be in," the First Minister continued through Marc's silence. "You are racking up quite the tab here."

"Rishad told us everything before he died," Marc reminded him. "Everything about the human experiments they were conducting at Vertellica. Why and how they used children and who was responsible." Marc put special emphasis on the last sentence.

For the first time during the conversation, First Minister Shen showed frustration.

"I'm not surprised. It's no secret that Rishad and I didn't agree on many issues. This, of course, was one of the biggest ones."

"He said that you both disagreed about how to live on the surface. And everything I saw explains why." Marc began to make his place in the conversation better known.

"Yes, Rishad was a fool. Any schooling scientist knows that terraforming a planet can take centuries. But yet he still pushed for it." First Minister Shen turned away from the glass to think. "'This is the safest way!' he would always say to me. Over and over and over again."

"And you didn't want to terraform." Marc commented, shaking his head in disbelief.

"Yes, I'm sure he told you that, keep up," First Minister Shen was getting frustrated remembering his arguments with Rishad. "I told him countless times, the only way we can truly live on the surface is if we adapt to it, rather than the other way around." He turned around again to collect himself and face Marc. "Sometimes a few must die for the benefit of the many."

"You sanctioned the human experiments," Marc said, still feeling his way through the new information. "Rishad hated the idea, so terraforming using plants was his plan!" He was getting the full picture now. *'He wanted what's best for everyone, no one above the rest.'* Marc remembered a few of Rishad's last words. Guilt grew inside of him.

First Minister Shen was recollecting his thoughts with an uncomfortable expression on his face. It was the first time Marc had seen him feel out of control.

"And now he's dead. And you killed him, Marc." On that note he turned around and walked away as the glass clouded with black. Marc was again alone with his thoughts. Guilt for Rishad's death filled him.

Why didn't Rishad tell us? Did he feel threatened by Aran? Thoughts raced around in Marc's head as he tried to find internal justification for what had happened. He couldn't find any. He paced around his tiny dark cell for hours until finally he sat on the floor, exhausted from the constant movement. His mind wasn't done moving.

Marc ran through his many interactions with First Minister Shen. He always seemed to want what was best for the people and was willing to do anything for them. But he always had a negative attitude towards Vertellica. Marc had always assumed it was because they conducted experiments he didn't think were right. Or because they wanted his power. It turns out that Vertellica tried to be the voice of reason, and that the First Minister was using his power to conduct horrible experiments.

Marc remembered his conversations with the First Minister. He always found a way to weave adaptation or evolution into conversations. He seemed so fond of the concept. It had never crossed Marc's mind that he wanted to force an entire population to adapt. That's why they were gradually lowering the oxygen levels in the colony.

Marc laid down on the hard floor and put his hands on his head. It all made sense now.

Several more hours passed when the glass wall cleared up again and First Minister Shen revealed himself. Marc stood up to meet his gaze.

"Marc," the First Minister began. "You were supposed to help me advance this colony. Not put its future on hold." He shook his head as he spoke.

"Did you think that I would just go along while you killed children?" Marc asked.

"Kill children? I looked at the data, Marc. That child was perfectly healthy until you ended the experiment." Marc felt his eyes stare deep inside him and the weight of the words hit his heart. "You killed that child."

Marc was speechless.

"Maybe understanding that will give you the motivation to decide to work with me," First Minister Shen said.

"So you're going to let me out of this cell?" Marc asked.

"That depends."

"On what?"

"On what you would do if I let you out," the First Minister concluded. "We were friends, after all. And we could be again."

"And what if I end up stirring up more trouble, or telling someone what was really going on?" Marc asked a dangerous question.

"The people of the Makan Colony will hear what you've done, Marc. No one will believe the word of a murderer," First Minister Shen said confidently.

"Tell me this, then," Marc started. "If the leader of Vertellica was against you, who was helping you do all this?"

"Now you're asking the important questions, Marc," the First Minister responded. "But I'm sure you've heard stories."

Marc stared back with confusion.

"Surely your friend Ashley told you what happened to her father?"

"He refused to do your experiments, and Vertellica fired him," Marc said, remembering his conversation in the Experience Plaza.

"Yes, and sad to say that he died shortly after," First Minister Shen smiled subtly to Marc.

"You killed him?"

"No," the First Minister said definitively. "But that's not to say I didn't take away his access to sufficient medical care and restrict his activity around the colony."

Marc was filled with dread. A good man's life, a father's life, was so restricted that he died because he wouldn't conduct research he didn't believe was right.

"Needless to say," First Minister Shen continued. "He was the last man to refuse to do the work I requested. Sure, Rishad gave me a hard time sometimes. But he was a smart man and I needed him around. And he knew what would happen if he didn't do the work I needed him for. He kept his workers motivated without the need for threats. And he knew I was in control."

"So then what's your plan with me?" Marc asked.

"I'm still figuring that out, Marc."

Suddenly, a hidden door opened into Marc's cell and a security guard shot a stunner into his chest.

Marc dropped to the floor as a dark cloud covered his eyes.

16

Marc awoke in a familiar setting. He looked around to see an empty lab. The same lab he and John had been working in at Vertellica. The same lab where Rishad died.

"Feeling alright?" Marc stood up from a hard-backed chair and turned around to see First Minister Shen standing and facing the Ridge of Daggers. The very ridge that killed Rishad. There were still dark stains where his blood fell. He turned to look at Marc. "I don't know if we've ever stunned someone twice in 24 hours before. I wasn't sure how your brain would hold up." He showed no emotion.

"What are we doing here?" Marc asked poignantly. His intensity was unmet by the apparent sorrow in the First Minister's face.

"Simply put, Marc," First Minister Shen began. "You've caused a lot of trouble here. We're here to see if you're worth it."

"And what if I'm not? You'll kill me?" Marc didn't show his fear. "Just like you're slowly killing everyone else?"

"We'll handle that situation, if necessary, but I'm not going to kill anyone," he responded. He walked towards Marc calmly. Marc studied his calculated movements.

"At least not by your own hand," Marc responded. He began to take an aggressive step towards First Minister Shen when he was grabbed by a WOSE security guard.

"You thought I would leave you in a chair, without restraints, and approach you alone? After you killed someone?" He laughed. "Maybe you're right. The lack of oxygen *is* getting to your brain." He laughed again while the security guard looked down at Marc with perplexed eyes. Marc recognized him as the same guard that escorted him to the Advisory Council meeting. He struggled against the strong Hexball player's grip.

"Now what?" Marc asked. He was worried now.

"Like I said, Marc, we're going to decide if you're worth the trouble."

"Are you going to push me onto the geotable just like Lian did to Rishad?" Marc looked at the stained table and then back to the First Minister who was moving in the opposite direction.

"Of course not," he responded.

"What's your plan then?" Marc looked around the lab, trying to look for clues.

"We're going to check out your research. See if it's making progress or not." He made his way towards the lockers on the other side of the room. The guard escorted Marc in the same direction. "Then we'll use that information to decide what to do with you."

"I see. I wouldn't expect to see much. Plants take time to grow." Marc was released as First Minister Shen began grabbing a suit and putting it on himself.

"I'll be honest, I'm hoping we find something good up there," he smiled as he pulled the flexible suit up his legs. The guard assisted him with some jumbled confusion.

Marc began pulling on his own suit. He zipped the suit up on his left side before pulling the flap over and zipping again up to his neck ring. Snapping the neck ring into a full circle, he looked to the First Minister, he was watching Marc closely.

"It's been a while since I've been to the surface," First Minister Shen admitted as if he was having a casual conversation with a friend.

"I've only been once," Marc continued the conversation. He placed his helmet on his head facing backwards. He then twisted it so the gold visor faced forward and then felt a click. He saw First Minister Shen following suit with the help of the guard. He seemed to copy Marc exactly. Marc tapped his wrist controller to turn on his microphone and he signaled for the First Minister to copy.

"Can you hear me?" Marc asked.

"Yes, am I coming through?"

"Yes," Marc said begrudgingly. He was getting tired of the laid-back attitude. It didn't match the situation.

"Marc, come and check my setup," First Minister Shen requested. "I'd hate to have a leak in my suit." He was holding his arms up and feeling around his helmet. Marc approached him and examined his suit. His helmet was tilted more off-center than Marc's own. He twisted closer to the center until he felt slight resistance and then a click.

"Should be all set," Marc said. "Your helmet wasn't sealed off." He saw First Minister Shen's eyebrows raise in surprise as he put his hands on the helmet.

"I didn't think you would actually help me," the First Minister said. Marc realized that it was a test. "Are you ready to proceed?" Marc gave no response. First Minister Shen approached the airlock door. He pulled down the lever to open the inner door and entered the small room.

Marc hesitated to follow but was helped along by the security guard who remained in the lab. He passed through the thin door behind the First Minister. Once the two were inside, Marc pulled the lever behind them to close the inner door.

"I really don't enjoy doing this, Marc," the First Minister was talking as he began to tap the screen by the outer door.

Marc was barely listening as he double checked his own suit.

"I had to get the airlock information from John, you know," First Minister Shen continued talking. "He had to walk me through everything so that I could get you out here if you refused to come. Of course he didn't know why." He turned to face Marc again as they waited.

The light above the outer door blinked green. Marc gestured at it and First Minister Shen turned around to pull the lever, opening the door to the surface. The two proceeded out as they stood looking at the landscape. The golden sun was setting over the mountains after the long day. The valley shadows were shifting and extending.

The light revealed a small, unexpected surprise. There was a row of small saplings protruding from the soil. The two stood without words.

Marc's situation became unknown to him as he approached the small green stems and kneeled next to them. He didn't pay attention to First Minister Shen, who grabbed a small set of garden shears from the toolbox. Marc brushed the thin plants through his covered hands, admiring the growth.

"This is incredible," he said, mostly talking to himself.

"This is certainly," First Minister Shen paused. "Unexpected." He had walked up next to Marc to examine the plants.

"They're actually growing," Marc said, full of wonder. "I didn't expect it to happen so soon. I thought they would fail to respire enough to maintain their metabolism, but John's work must've done more than expected."

"This certainly proves something correct," First Minister Shen began. "Life from Earth can be adapted to live on this surface, even without terraforming."

Marc rose quickly to look at him.

"These plants were engineered to survive this; they weren't forced to adapt like the children in your failed experiments." Marc was filled with rage. He couldn't believe the First Minister's takeaway.

"I can't deny that this work was very useful, Marc. But how we use the information will be up to me and whoever I place in charge of Vertellica. We've been looking after this colony since long before you got here, and we know what's best for the future here."

"You're going to destroy this colony," Marc said. "Don't you see what this means? We can grow plants here which means we can plant forests to produce oxygen. It won't be overnight, but within decades we could make the surface of this small planet habitable." Marc's estimate was exaggerated to reassure the First Minister of his value.

"The only thing this proves is that it's possible," First Minister Shen said. "You have no idea how long it would take, or even if this will work with other plants." Marc was shaking his head and had to walk away. The First Minister had to clear his throat. "No, we will continue to evolve the people here to prepare them."

Suddenly Marc felt the force of something cutting through the back of his suit. First Minister Shen used the shears to breach it.

Marc stumbled as he turned around and realized what had happened. He nearly fell on one of the saplings.

"What are you doing?!" he exclaimed, feeling his suit for the tear.

"I told you, Marc. If I thought you were worth the trouble, I'd keep you around. But I've decided that's not the case." The First Minister stood over Marc, looking down at his black suit.

Marc's hands fumbled in the soil around him until he grabbed a solid handle. He jumped to his feet and sliced at First Minister Shen's suit. Using his metal hori hori to cut a hole into it.

The First Minister leaned back and dropped the shears. His hands grasped at the hole Marc carved into his suit.

"I'm trying to do this for the good of the human race!" he yelled and began to move away from Marc. He started to move back towards the airlock.

"They're not even going to be humans anymore!" Marc yelled. "You're going to fundamentally change people, physiologically and mentally so that they're a completely different species of beings." He followed First Minister Shen and saw his right hand against his chest.

"I don't understand, Marc." He shook one of his arms as the knife fell from his hand. "I thought you were smart, but I don't understand your logic."

"It's basic evolution," Marc started again with a cough. "If an organism changes enough, it branches off to become a new species." There was silence for a brief time while the two moved towards the airlock. The First Minister's coughing came through clearly on the speakers in Marc's helmet, despite his own coughing.

"But they're still humans," First Minister Shen responded, his helmet cocked with confusion. "Just better adapted." He continued to cough. He was at the airlock now, and Marc went in the door right behind him.

The First Minister put his hand on the latch to close the door, but before he could pull down, Marc grabbed the latch to keep the door open.

"I told you, First Minister. Forcing people to live with less oxygen isn't safe."

There was no response as First Minister Shen was shaking one of his hands, trying to pull the latch despite Marc's opposition.

"What are you doing?" First Minister Shen said. The sound of gasping came through the speaker in Marc's suit. "We'll both die."

"No," Marc responded, coughing, but speaking clearly. "Only you."

"Why?" the First Minister asked in a barely audible groan. He dropped to his knees. Marc kneeled down in front of him.

"You've been spending most of your time in your residence where you have 21 percent oxygen," Marc answered. "And I've been adjusting to 17 percent."

"How?" First Minister Shen could barely get the word out.

"*Rafflesia aerobia*," Marc explained.

A groan was the only response.

"Sometimes a few must die for the benefit of the many," Marc said, putting his hand on First Minister Shen's shoulder to keep him upright. "You told me that. Do you remember?"

The gasping sounds were much quieter now.

First Minister Shen's body collapsed to the side. Marc stood over him as he looked down through his gold translucent visor. There was little movement in the collapsed body. Hypoxia had done its work.

Marc reached up and pulled the airlock latch down. He coughed and coughed as the door shut and he collapsed. His vision faded away.

17

Marc's eyes slowly blinked open, revealing a bright room around him.

"Marc, you're awake!" Greg leaned over him. Marc realized he was in a bed in the medbay. He recounted his memories from the airlock and sat up.

"How are you feeling?" Greg asked.

"I'm fine, I think," came Marc's slow response.

"Security said that you and First Minister Shen were on the surface lab but when the airlock unsealed neither of you came out. The guy said that you two were both lying unconscious with holes in your suits." Greg studied Marc's face for a sign of what might have happened.

"Yeah."

"What happened?" Greg asked.

"I…" Marc paused. "Don't remember."

"Well, I'm just glad you're alright. You're doing better than the First Minister, that's for sure."

"How is he?" Marc asked, not sure what answer he was hoping for.

"The Docs say he's not going to die, but it's hard to tell how much damage has been done. As far as they can tell, his brain activity is minimal. Seems like he might be in a permanent coma." Marc nodded in acknowledgment.

"Greg," Marc began. "Have you seen John or Ashley?"

"Yes, I saw them earlier today in WOSE containment," he admitted.

"He had us in some kind of holding cells. He said that we killed Rishad and that we were going to spend a long time there." Marc watched Greg's reaction to see how much he knew.

"I know that none of you meant to kill Rishad," Greg said, putting his hand on Marc's shoulder. "I saw the security footage before Vertellica took it away."

"Can you try to get John and Ashley out?"

Suddenly, the two came into the room smiling.

"Good to see you, Marc," John said. Ashley leaned into his bed to give him a hug.

"I'm glad you're all okay," Marc said, looking around the room. Another thought crossed his mind.

"Lian is in the medbay with First Minister Shen," Greg read his mind. "Unfortunately, she is going to be confined to her residence for a while, outside of visits to her father, of course. She did physically assault a Vertellica representative and they're deciding if they want to charge her with involuntary manslaughter."

"What about us?" Ashley asked.

"I talked to them; we went through the footage. The people at Vertellica could see that you didn't want to hurt Rishad."

"I can't say I didn't think about it," John admitted. "With the research he was conducting. It was terrible."

Greg and Ashley both nodded in silent agreement.

"Rishad was opposed to the experiments," Marc told them. "He only wanted to terraform and always argued with the First Minister about it." Ashley's eyes widened.

"You mean Rishad was on our side?" she showed a mix of surprise and sadness.

"Yes," came the solemn answer.

"I should've known," John sat down with a grave face. "He never seemed like the type to do something that terrible. He didn't hide anything from us when we asked."

"No one knew what was going to happen," Marc tried to console him. "It was really the First Minister that was manipulating everyone. He made people do the research, and threatened them if they refused. Just like he did to Ashley's father years ago." He looked at her.

Ashley closed her eyes to prevent tears from dripping down her face.

"And he tried to kill me on the surface lab," Marc added decidedly. Eyebrows around the room raised.

"So then what now?" John asked, keeping the big picture in mind.

"First Minister Shen is in a coma. So he seems to be out of the picture. However that happened." Greg put the pieces together but didn't care to share his understanding with everyone.

"If he was oxygen deprived long enough to go into a coma, he probably won't come out of it. Too much brain damage." John added his knowledge, maintaining his somber mood.

"So we don't have a First Minister?" Ashley asked.

"Or a Vertellica Head," Greg added, looking at John.

"The First Minister will be voted in at the next Advisory Council meeting," John said. "We will have an internal meeting at Vertellica for our position."

"Are you going to get it?" Marc asked.

"We'll see how people treat me after the recent events, but I think there could be a chance. Whoever is in charge, I guarantee there won't be any more human experiments going on. And our surface project will continue to progress."

Ashley smiled, still sad but relieved.

"Who knows, maybe Greg could even become First Minister," Marc added with a subtle smile.

"First Minister Andino," Ashley said. "Has a nice ring to it."

"I guess anything could happen," Greg grinned thinking about the potential promotion.

"Regardless, we can fix the colony's oxygen level," John said. Marc took a moment for himself to think.

"We can't," he said finally.

"What do you mean?" Greg asked. "Didn't you say the low oxygen level was harmful."

"It was likely the reason that five people died in the last year," Marc admitted.

"Then why can't we fix it?" Ashley asked, dumbfounded.

"Remember what happened when we tried to save the child, John?" Marc asked. John nodded silently with dark eyes of despair.

"Raising the oxygen level too high would kill more people than leaving it alone," Marc said in a calculated voice. "First Minister Shen was right, people are adapting."

ACKNOWLEDGMENTS

The journey of *Makan* has been an evolution, and I owe a debt of gratitude to everyone who supported this project across its different iterations.

I want to extend a heartfelt thank you to Crypsis Press. Thank you for welcoming *Makan* into your catalog and giving it such a beautiful new home. Taking this story to the next level under the Crypsis banner has been an incredible experience, and I couldn't have asked for a better partner in this new chapter of my writing career.

To my family, friends, and early readers: your feedback and encouragement kept me writing when the science got complicated and the mysteries got dark. This book belongs to you as much as it does to me.

STAY CONNECTED

Stay Connected with Evan Couchot

Whether it's unearthing ancient folklore horror, deconstructing a complex mystery, or exploring the far reaches of science fiction, Evan's work explores the darker side of human behavior. Join Evan's personal newsletter for updates on the ongoing work, behind-the-scenes research, and news on upcoming releases across all genres. **Join the Author's Circle at www.CrypsisPress.com**

The Crypsis Collective

Crypsis Press LLC is more than a publisher—it is a mission to build better worlds through fiction. By joining the **Crypsis Collective**, you'll gain access to the official press newsletter, featuring first-look reveals at our expanding catalog, limited edition announcements, and exclusive community content. **Enter the Crypsis Collective at www.Crypsis-Press.com**

About the Author

Evan Couchot lives at the intersection of what we know and what we fear. From the quiet streets of Mason, Ohio, to the laboratories of Boston, his work is defined by a fascination with the natural world and the mechanics of life.

As a biotechnology professional with degrees in Biology and Biotechnology, Evan brings a high degree of technical realism to his fiction. His stories—spanning deep-space science fiction, folklore mystery, and pharmaceutical-themed thrillers—are rooted in a deep understanding of the living world. Evan currently lives and works in Boston, where the city's history and innovation provide constant inspiration for his next mystery.

Also By Evan Couchot

NOVELS:

Adverse Events (coming 2026)

NOVELLAS:

Insatiable

9 781971 827032